America Di Utopian

T0274421

Written by Kenneth C. Bible

Co written by Jeffrey Bible and Martha Bible

Dedication

I would like to dedicate this book to my grandfathers. Ideologically, they are diametrically opposed to each other, but I love each of them and have learned much from both of them. Grandpa Bible served in the United States Air Force for twenty-four years, willing to sacrifice his life for a better tomorrow for our country, ending his time as a Master Sergeant. He is a straight-up, no-nonsense, tell it like it is person, politically considered to be on the right. He loves this nation and would do anything to preserve it for his grandchildren and beyond. Grandpa Naugle, on the other hand, was a teacher for twenty-eight years, much of the time as a special education teacher, teaching and helping emotionally disabled students. He is considered to be on the left politically, but he, too, is willing to and has put his life on the line to create a better tomorrow for his grandchildren and his country. As the recipient of their pearls of wisdom, these two people have had a profound effect on my understanding of the complicated political continuum of the United States.

Kenneth C. Bible

Disclaimer

This is a work of fiction. Unless otherwise indicated, all the names, characters, businesses, places, events, and incidents in this book are either the product of the authors' imaginations or used in a fictitious manner. Any resemblance to actual persons, living or dead, or actual events, is purely coincidental.

Table of Contents

CHAPTER ONE

INTRODUCTION

Our story begins in the fall of 2036, at the end of the Presidential election cycle. In a special documentary recorded prior to the final debate, one of the news networks shows a series of events which have shaped the rich history of the United States. Some of these "Events in History" predate the birth of this nation.

The show opens up with a flat world map shown. Intense, dark piano music is playing. The screen then divides into four sections. The left twenty-five percent of the screen shows a list of events. Each event on the list is highlighted as its enactment is being shown. To the right of the list, the screen is divided into three sections. Taking up the majority of the screen is a series of maps and pictures, with a magnifying glass going to each event as the listed item is being highlighted. Below this panorama, as each event is shown, the two candidates, President Isaac Wolfe and his challenger Texas Governor Jim Taylor, give their comments, which are shown only in writing but are voiced over. President Wolfe always goes first, whose comments are shown in white text against a blue background on the left, then Governor Taylor, whose comments are shown in white against a red background on the right.

Here is the list of historical events which are shown in this documentary:

1. Pilgrims coming to the New World to find freedom of religion and freedom from tyranny, yet maintaining their British identity
2. Boston Tea Party
3. Signing of the Declaration of Independence
4. Revolutionary War
5. Signing of the United States Constitution
6. 1861, Introduction of a US Income Tax to fund the Civil War

7. Political and military maps of WWI Europe, followed by newspaper headlines of the US defeating Germany

8. 1935, FDR signing the Social Security Act

9. 1944, WWII D-Day, and FDR's prayer calling for all Americans to remain in prayer for "our sons" to have "stoutness of heart" and "steadfastness in their faith" in order to "set free a suffering humanity"

10. Newspaper headlines showing the Allies winning WWII

11. 1956, President Eisenhower announcing the Federal Highway Act

12. 1962, Cuban Missile Crisis

13. 1973, Energy Crisis

14. 1987, President Reagan's speech demanding USSR General Secretary Mikhail Gorbachev to "Tear down this wall!"

15. 9/11

16. Health care crisis and the Affordable Healthcare Act signed into law by President Obama

Scene 1: Pilgrims

Isaac

The pilgrims are considered heroes for their rebellion against the Crown, but this act was treasonous. Not only that, but they endangered their own children, as many of them died, and for what, a false sense of a better life? It can only be considered a pure case of child endangerment; why, if the Natives hadn't taught them how to survive, they all would have died!

Jim

THIS is what America is all about! People fought for freedom. They sacrificed their lives and everything they had for the future of their children and their children's children. Leaving a tyrannical government and oppression behind, they fought on for their British identity but with the freedom to live according to their religious beliefs and with the simple liberties that *every* human is entitled to *by God*. Better to be dead than to live without freedom. As the great American patriot Patrick Henry said, "Give me liberty or give me death!"

Scene 2: Boston Tea Party

Isaac

What a terrible moment in history! The Boston Tea Party was nothing more than rebellion against the established government, which was only trying to *help* its citizens. And, to top it off, just think of how badly these people polluted the harbor that night by dumping all that tea into it. There's no telling what their actions did to the marine life!

Jim

Another great moment in American history, the Boston Tea Party was a perfect way to fight the oppression of overzealous government, with its taxation without representation – a great display of American problem solving!

Scene 3: Declaration of Independence

Isaac

The final blow to our heritage, disavowing our family, it took generations after this to rebuild diplomacy with England, our Motherland. This should have never happened. Our forefathers didn't give diplomacy a chance. Had they tried a little harder, we would still be part of the United Kingdom today, and all of those deaths could have been avoided – very sad, *very* sad!

Jim

This brings a tear to my eyes. They had faith, will power, and determination to be free, to let no government rule the people. This they did at the risk of everything they had, even their very lives! Our forefathers tried every avenue available to them to persuade King George to be reasonable, but the power-hungry Monarch refused, leaving them no choice but to break free from his tyranny. They sacrificed so much so that *we* can be free today.

Scene 4: Revolutionary War

Isaac

How could they revolt against the Crown, after Mother England had allowed them to live in North America, and even sent supplies to help them? Another very sad moment in human history, this was like a son turning his back on his parents after all the love and care they gave him – a travesty really!

Jim

A great deed done by our forefathers, they fought off the oppressive English government. This was the vital step necessary to form a government *of* the people, *by* the people, and *for* the people, the very foundation of a free world. Freedom is *worth* the price of death! I thank God for those people and for the freedom to stand here before you today as a direct result of their actions to break away from that tyrant, King George III!

Scene 5: U. S. Constitution

Isaac

Finally, our ancestors were thinking right! A marvelous piece of work for that time, the US Constitution *was* very relevant for its day, and it continued to be up until relatively modern times. Although it is outdated today and needs to abolished, it was a great work that lasted over 250 years.

Jim

Aside from the Holy Bible, this is perhaps the most important document in the history of the world, a timeless law of the land. The United States Constitution is adaptable by amendments and is the basis of a free world. It should be able to stand another ten millennia and still rule our great country well. Yet again, we see amazing work done by our forefathers!

Scene 6: Civil War & Introduction of a Federal Income Tax

Isaac

What a wonderful event in American history! President Lincoln took a little money from everyone, for the *good* of everyone. Although the majority of citizens believe this great first step toward evening out our economic inequality took place in 1913, we actually have *everyone's* favorite President Abraham Lincoln to thank for the introduction of a tiny 3-5% *progressive* income tax in order to pay for the Civil War. It was the redistribution of wealth, the very foundation of a utopian society.

Jim

What was Lincoln thinking, introducing the Federal Income Tax?! Why, I can tell you what he was thinking. President Lincoln cleverly waited until Congress went on break to declare war on the Confederate States. I don't disagree that the cause to end slavery was just and noble, *but*, he set a *terrible* precedent for future Presidents to follow to tax-and-spend, abuse their position, and usurp authority over Congress and the American people. This was the very start of Big Government. President Lincoln took the first step towards socialism by proposing to his cabinet members that Americans pay income tax to cover the financial costs of the Civil War.

Scene 7: WWI

Isaac

We should *never* have gone to war! We had no right to govern other nations or influence their ways. President Wilson should have heeded the Germans' warning to stay out of the war zones. Although Europeans wildly cheered the idea of going to war in the beginning, it was simply inexcusable to forego the pursuit of diplomacy, which could have spared all of those victims from this horrendous event! Millions of lives were either lost or irreparably damaged because of "The Great War." It was a great tragedy that could have, and *should* have, been prevented diplomatically. Unfortunately, it was only after World War I ended that President Wilson took steps to build a League of Nations.

Jim

What a time for America – "the Land of the Free and the Home of the Brave!" Our free nation fought for *world* freedom, to help *billions* of people worldwide to achieve the goal of a free world! Oh, what a great country we live in, that will always answer the call to help any nation in the pursuit of freedom.

Scene 8: Social Security Act

Isaac

What a great time in American history. Why, what a great man was FDR, the greatest U.S. President of all time, standing up for the people and giving them a government that will actually take care of them! Social Security, unemployment, and welfare were all rolled up into one tidy bill. This is the greatest act of legislation in American history. Here, we see the start of a caring, nurturing government *for* the people. This was exactly what the people needed then and still need today.

Jim

Our senior citizens should not be left without the basic necessities of life, but it is the responsibility of every individual and then that person's family, to take care of them. It is not only their responsibility; it is the *right* of a person to take pride in their own being and to *work* to provide for themselves and their family. This was the biggest step toward socialism in our country, and it is exactly *why* we fought against England. It is a basic human right to work to live and pursue happiness. Because of this one act, Americans today are paying over 70% of their paychecks in taxes, which is *far* worse than even the Boston Tea Party participants ever had to deal with. A bloated government is just not right, not good at all. This is what started government control. Oh, what a *terrible* time in American history! People have become dependent upon the government, and the government, then, has power over their lives. Much freedom was lost on that fateful day, my friends – indeed a *sad* day in American history!

Scene 9: D-Day/FDR Asking Americans to Pray

Isaac

Here, we see another sad day in American history. Burdened for years by the effects of polio and the pressures of being President, FDR became unraveled. His warmongering advisors took advantage of his frail state and convinced him to go to war, because a few American lives were taken by Japan. It was a war that we had no business to be in, as there was still time for diplomacy to work. Let me be absolutely clear: we have *no* right to interfere in the governments of other nations! FDR was so exhausted by the war, his health just gave out. He could have lived another decade or two, if we would have just left well enough alone and stayed out of it. What a *terrible* loss to America!

Jim

(Audibly sniffling and holding back tears) It took years to plan it, and Churchill tried to persuade President Roosevelt to take a peripheral strategy, but D-Day, the culmination of FDR's Grand Strategy, became the single proudest moment in American history. That night, FDR gave his famous speech, in which he humbly prayed for God to "lead (our sons) straight and true; give strength to their arms, stoutness to their hearts, steadfastness in their faith," in order to "set free a suffering humanity." D-Day was the beginning of the defeat of Hitler and his Nazi Party. Americans were proud to serve and volunteered to help their nation. Famous athletes and people from *all* walks of life joined the fight, of their own free will. No draft was really needed. Americans were proud to serve their God, family, and country. Freedom always wins out. It always has, and it always will, as long as people are willing to fight for it.

Scene 10: America Wins WWII

Isaac

Win? They said we won, but at what cost? At what cost, really, did we win? Look at all the millions of lives that were lost and all the families that were affected. The United States actually released two atomic bombs on our Japanese friends. Oh, the shame, the *horrific shame* – this should have never ever happened, and it could have all been avoided if more emphasis had been given to peaceful solutions!

Jim

U-S-A! U-S-A! We saved the world again, for the second time in thirty years. What a great country we live in: we rid the world of the most evil human being in all of history! Because of us, Hitler was not able to succeed. Our love of *freedom* once again saved the world.

Scene 11: Federal Highway Act of 1956

Isaac

This is one of the few things the other party did right. They understood the benefits of government rule, uniting American workers under one project – a project designed, implemented, and paid for by the Federal Government. Private enterprise and the thirst for personal wealth are just *not capable* of a feat such as this. We had to learn from Germany the importance of government taking over this part of society, for society's own benefit.

Jim

A perfect example of the trickle-down effect, the building of highways for our national defense allowed the troops to go cross-country in a matter of weeks instead of months. It was a *brilliant* move! American taxpayers invested $25 billion on this project, and for years, it has provided many jobs to the American workforce and rapid commerce, which strengthened our economy, not only then, but also today.

Scene 12: Cuban Missile Crisis

Isaac

How close we came to an all out nuclear war, and for what? We had no business being involved in the Bay of Pigs, and we certainly had no business telling Cuba what they could and could not do. Besides, we, unfortunately, had nuclear missiles in Europe pointing to Russia. Why couldn't Russia have the same liberty? It's not our place to tell another government what it can and cannot do, but because of arrogance, we almost ended the human race with an all out nuclear war!

Jim

No way could we let Cuba have nukes! That island is way too close to the United States' borders. They could have destroyed us in less than an hour. No, not in this hemisphere, there should *never* be nukes pointing to us in our hemisphere! I can't believe that Kennedy would even negotiate our taking nuclear missiles out of Italy and Turkey for an agreement for them to keep missiles out of Cuba. We lost on this deal. What a show of weakness, and we paid for it for many years with the threat of a Russian nuclear attack, based on *our* weakness.

Scene 13: 1973, Energy Crisis

Isaac

This was just *terrible* diplomacy! We had no right to invoke the anger of our Arabic allies by defending Israel. We unwisely chose to enter *their* conflict, and the Arabs had every right to keep *their* oil from *us*. With that being said, President Nixon showed great wisdom by appointing an Energy Czar to ration the States' amounts of oil. The government stepped in and made things better by controlling the situation – a situation which, once again, private enterprise could not handle.

Jim

When the Arabs attacked our ally, our *friend*, Israel, it was an act of war. Not only should we have retaliated on Israel's behalf, but we should have captured Arabic oil fields and conquered their territory to put an end to the Middle Eastern terrorism. That would have solved this problem, and 9/11, the greatest attack on American soil, would *never* have happened. We could have brought peace to the region and prosperity to their people, many of whom still live in third world status to this day. The opportunity was lost for them, for the United States, and for the world.

Scene 14: President Reagan's Speech

Isaac

We had no business telling Russia how to govern their people. The US didn't need to be bullying other countries around. This behavior only caused terrorism against our country, and it is why the world hated us.

Jim

What a great speech, and what a great day in American history! All of Reagan's advisors told him not to say it. In fact, his speech writers took it out of his speech, but you can't stop a great American. "Tear down this wall, tear down this wall!"

Scene 15: 9/11

Isaac

September 11th was our own fault, ladies and gentlemen, because of our continuous, arrogant meddling and support of Israel in a religious dispute that was not even ours. It never was, nor should it ever be. The Arabs hate us even today because of this, and rightly so. How *dare* we try to influence those cultures, a whole ocean away? We have no right to any say-so in that land, and if I were them, I would hate us too. I'm surprised more violence hasn't erupted against the US. They are actually showing great restraint!

Jim

(Gritting his teeth and taking a deep breath before he speaks) This angers me to no end. How could we let this happen? We should have taken over that territory in '73, and we should have never, *ever*, let them do *this* to us! Japan killed fewer Americans in their attack on Pearl Harbor, and what did we do to them? We *nuked* them, *twice*! But what did we do to retaliate against the Arabs? Basically *nothing*, and look, today we don't have the freedoms we had before this event! Think about it. We still have to take our shoes and belts off every time we go to the airport, and the police can search any of us at any time, for any reason, and just say they *think* a person is a terrorist. Unbelievable! (Jim takes another deep breath.) How can we go on like this? We *must* put an end to this tyranny, once and for all. Freedom *is* worth fighting for, because if you're not free, you might as well be dead!

Scene 16: ObamaCare

Isaac

What a great President, Barack Hussein Obama, Jr., my favorite President of this century! When he took office, twenty percent of Americans were uninsured, and for those who were insured, preexisting conditions were not covered, making it more like thirty-five percent without coverage. The situation needed to be changed, and this *outstanding* President was clever enough, and determined enough, to adopt a plan much like that of our Canadian friends, to give healthcare to everyone. After all, it is the government's duty to take care of its people, and this great man pushed the necessary legislation through, despite heavy opposition. President Obama is my second favorite leader in *all* of *history*, following closely behind FDR!

Jim

Such a dark time in American history, yet another socialistic act was forced upon the American public. Healthcare is a job better suited to free enterprise. The government cannot, and should not, dictate to the people who should be insured. And look how it took off, from requiring insurance, to government doctors now determining who lives and who dies, who is on a waiting list and who gets immediate attention. This is un-American, and it goes *completely* against the Constitution, which guarantees the *right* to *life*, as well as liberty and the pursuit of happiness to *all*.

END CHAPTER

CHAPTER TWO

FINAL DEBATE AND REACTIONS

As the election cycle winds down, the final Presidential Debate is held at a university in Washington. The date of this event is October 28, 2036. It is a much anticipated event, as the very existence of the United States is at stake. Many people are acutely aware of how their lives will be completely changed in the upheaval that could soon take place.

The debate features two candidates, the moderator, and an audience. The moderator opens the debate excitedly: "Welcome to the third and final Presidential Debate, here in Washington, just one week before the election on November 4th. Based on the drastic change in government on the ballot, this may be the very most important debate ever held in history of the United States. As you know, if President Isaac Wolfe is voted in for his third term, we will abolish all future elections and nullify the United States Constitution, along with our current form of government, and we will become a socialist nation under the leadership of 'Czar Wolfe.'" He pauses for a moment and then continues with his introduction: "And, if Governor Jim Taylor wins, we get a new President. President Wolfe, as the incumbent President, you have the honor of going first. Our opening question tonight is: 'If you are elected, what are your plans for the first few months of transition?' In other words, what will it be like?"

Jim quickly interrupts the moment before Isaac has had a chance to speak: "Yes, Mr. President, what *will* it be like for the American people?"

The moderator, who is annoyed with Jim's impolite behavior, patiently redirects the attention back to the President with the reprimand, "It's not your turn to speak, Governor. Please follow the debate rules." Jim apologizes, and the moderator continues before turning the microphone over to Isaac: "Please, Mr. President, let's hear your thoughts."

Isaac begins to speak immediately: "Well, I would like to begin by thanking everyone here in the state of Washington, and everyone at this university and everyone involved in this debate. And thank you, sir, for agreeing to moderate this debate."

The moderator happily answers him, "My pleasure, Mr. President!"

Isaac then goes on to answer the question: "Well, it won't be perfect, but it will be exciting! Changing from capitalism to socialism is a natural process, as Karl Marx and Friedrich Engels explained to us in *The Communist Manifesto*. But, it will require logistics. For example, the government will have to seize control of private enterprise, and we will have to appoint government employees to run everything. This is going to be a huge transition, but it is one that needs to be made, and it will be an exciting time in American history! In order to be most beneficial to society, the government will place everyone in the job that best suits their abilities, thus eliminating the oftentimes stressful decision of which career path to choose and, worse yet, joblessness. We will also be instituting a 250-square-foot maximum living space for each person, thereby eliminating homelessness. Every single individual and every family will be placed in homes to match their needs. Of course, all guns will be taken away, and all the necessities, such as food and gas, will be rationed so that everyone will have the same status and wealth. All money will be seized by the government and rendered worthless, so that everyone will finally have equal status and be happy. I have been working on this plan for the last seven years, and I believe it can and will be executed perfectly by my outstanding staff, with minimal disruptions to the lives of American citizens."

The audience cheers wildly, and the moderator works to calm down the crowd. "Bravo, Mr. President, this sounds like a perfect plan! Governor Taylor, you have two minutes to comment."

Jim is greatly disappointed by the crowd's reaction and addresses them: "Has everyone lost their minds? This is *communism*! This is what Russia did. The United States is built on freedoms: freedom of religion and freedom to pursue life, liberty, and happiness."

Isaac interrupts Jim, "That *is* what we are giving everyone." The audience cheers even more wildly, giving Isaac a standing ovation.

Jim continues with his rebuttal: "Excuse me, it's *my* turn now." The audience surprisingly becomes calm and sits down.

The moderator points out, "You have thirty seconds left, Governor."

Jim continues: "We cannot move to a socialist society; it's not in our genetics. We have always been rebels. From fleeing tyranny in the Church to fleeing tyranny in England, we are made to be a free people. We will not survive the turn to socialism. America, I plead with you, do not allow this so-called liberal, socialist, communistic agenda to be passed next week! Vote for me, vote for America, vote for your freedom!"

Jim's response, including interruptions, takes 2-1/2 minutes, so the moderator reprimands him again, saying: "You went over your two-minute allotment, Governor Taylor. I should not have to remind you again. Please follow the time clock to your left. You went over, and this will not be tolerated."

Time passes, and the moderator offers another question: "Ok, Governor, for the next question, you will start first. President Wolfe, you will then have two minutes to comment. The question is: 'We know that under President Wolfe's plan, unemployment will be eliminated, as everyone will be given a job, working for the government. What will you do for the unemployed if you are elected?'"

Jim answers with: "There's always a percentage of people, outliers, who just don't *want* to work. That's 3% of Americans who will *never want* to work. Those are statistics. My plan is to have an economy that will grow by providing jobs for everyone who wants them and to bring manufacturing back to companies owned in the US, and to stop this import garbage that has ruined our country. American businessmen and -women taking pride in their country and bringing jobs and ownership back to America, not because the government tells them to, but because they *want* to. *That* will result in a restoration of American pride. If we restore our people's faith in this great country, we will also make things happen *here*. Businesses will make money *here*, and foreign businesses will want to *come* here and negotiate to do business with American-owned companies. We have the greatest land in the world. We have oil, cotton, and good crops, *everything* we need to be self-sufficient. This is a land blessed by God, for God-fearing people who love this country. God, country, and family: that's what this great nation is all about!"

The moderator turns from Jim to Isaac and tells him, "Mr. President, you have two minutes, sir, to comment."

Isaac turns to Jim and asks, "Governor Taylor, how *dare* you say that 3% of Americans *just don't want to work*? What right do you have to judge their hearts and what they feel? The reason we have unemployment is that free enterprise is a failed system. Everyone wants to work and do a good job. The problem is, the rich business owners and managers take from the poor and work people too many hours a week, on the shades of slave labor, so that they don't have to hire more Americans, and so they can pad their pockets and laugh at the plight of less affluent people." The audience interrupts Isaac with wild cheering and a standing ovation. Isaac motions for the people to be seated, but the cheering goes on for approximately thirty seconds, and then the audience returns to their seats. "Under my system, everyone will only work seven hours a day, five days a week. The only people working on the

weekends will be emergency personnel, such as doctors."
Although he is nearing the two minute mark, Isaac continues:
"This will allow for peace and happiness for all, the pure
Utopian Society. Furthermore, as I mentioned previously,
there will be no unemployment, as the government will assign
a job to every single person." (The clock shows more than two
minutes have passed, and Jim points to the clock. The
moderator shakes his head at Jim.) Isaac continues
uninterrupted: "Governor Taylor is right in that we do have a
self-sufficient land, but we need to have a central point of
authority, which will be the federal government, in order to
fully utilize our great resources. We should not only share
these with everyone in our country, but also with the world.
We will have pride back in our country alright. Everyone will
love their country, and the world will love us. It's a win-win."

Jim shakes his head in response to Isaac's lack of
timeliness. Isaac's response, including interruptions, takes
approximately 3-1/2 minutes. The moderator is absolutely
thrilled by Isaac's response and thanks him for sharing his
great insight.

The debate continues on for a little while. Eventually,
the moderator asks Isaac about the national deficit, prefacing
the question with observations regarding the hopelessness of
the situation. "The deficit, I know, nobody wants to talk about
it. We're getting close to $100 quadrillion in debt, and our
credit rating is," pausing to take a breath, "gone. We are on the
verge of financial collapse. What can your new government do
to bring us out of this mess?"

Isaac gives an unexpectedly cheerful response: "That's
the beauty of a socialistic society. All resources are pooled
together under the government's control, including money and
employment. We will naturally work our way out of our debts,
which I believe we need to honor, to the rest of the world.
Everyone will make the equivalent of $35,000 a year, and the
government will give the people everything they need, based

on rations. All extra money from exports will go toward paying down the debt, so we should be debt-free within ten years. After that, we can take the extra money to help the rest of the world move toward a utopian society. My dream is to have Utopian Earth in twenty years, where everyone in the world will share equal status, with the same living conditions, the perfect world." The audience stands and applauds, lasting approximately thirty seconds. "Thank you, thank you all! I appreciate your support." Isaac's portion, including the interruption, lasts approximately ninety seconds.

The moderator shares the overwhelming feeling of relief with the audience and exclaims, "How very poetic – thank you, Mr. President!" Then, turning to Jim, he cannot help but feel depressed at the thought of more of the same and says to Jim with a heavy heart, "Governor Taylor, you have two minutes to respond, if you wish."

Jim's response is quite surprising to the moderator: "*If I WISH?!* Of course, I wish! I can't believe what is going on right in front of my eyes! This is NOT America. Everyone make $35,000? A doctor who goes to school for seven years and survives internship for four more, makes $35,000, while the janitor who played video games all his life and never sought improvement makes the same? Are you crazy? What is the incentive for someone to work hard and get ahead in life? It is that very incentive, to get ahead in life, which causes people to invent things. Creating new technologies, making the world better through innovation, and solving problems have traditionally been financially rewarded in this country. People become great because they are driven to make a better life for themselves and their children."

Isaac interrupts Jim's response with, "People will do these things simply to improve the world. Do you think Thomas Edison invented the light bulb for personal gain?"

Jim, who is getting angrier all the time, replies: "Isaac, are you that naive? Look at the patents that Edison held. He was a businessman, pure and simple. This was the free enterprise system at work! Edison was a good American trying to improve his life, and we have a light bulb because of it. Free enterprise system at work is how we have cars, TVs, microwaves, *all* the modern inventions. These are the things that allow us to live as kings only dreamed of living years ago. We prosper because of our drive to better our lives. We are enabled by freedom and driven by greed! It works. It may not be perfect, but it works. It's the best system around, and it's based on FREEDOM. We will not be told by the government what to do and when to do it, because it's the *right* of *every* American to work hard and give our kids a better life than we ever dreamed of having." Jim is interrupted by the moderator pointing to the clock. He looks at the moderator, then the clock, and then turns forward to address the audience again, saying: "This is free enterprise, the American dream. I beg you, America, do *not* let this man take away these freedoms, which every human being is entitled by God to enjoy!" Jim's response, including interruptions, took 2-1/2minutes.

The moderator tells Jim, "Governor Taylor, you went over by thirty seconds. Once again, Governor, please try to keep your responses brief!" The debate draws closer to its conclusion when the moderator asks the final question to Isaac. "If elected, what will happen to the relics of the past, like the Constitution, the Liberty Bell, and the Statue of Liberty? Will you keep these items as tourist attractions or put them in a museum? What are your plans, Mr. President?"

Isaac responds with an answer most disturbing to Jim: "The Statue of Liberty, I would give back to France. The Declaration of Independence and Constitution, I would burn in a ceremony a week after I'm elected. I would televise this to the whole world as an act of good faith. As for the Liberty Bell, we would just 'make that (crack) a little bigger,' to quote President Reagan. Then, we would melt it down and recycle it.

You see, these are mementos of a flawed government. They must be destroyed and or removed for a utopian society to exist. We must not keep these reminders of such an evil society that has caused *so* much grief to its people and to the world. Think of all the lives that were lost because of these items and what they represent. This is no better than the Crusades, senseless killing under the disguise of freedom. I will not let the American people suffer under this false deity of freedom any longer. These will be abolished, and a pure utopian system will emerge."

The audience and moderator stand and cheer wildly; the moderator has a tear in his eye as he makes his final remarks: "And that ends tonight's debate. Thank you, America, and remember to vote one week from tonight, and have yourselves a great evening!"

Isaac turns to shake Jim's hand but is only greeted with, "I'm not shaking your hand, you traitor! You are going to *burn* the Constitution? You cannot get away with this. You simply cannot be allowed to win this election. I cannot let this happen, and I will not allow it!"

Coldly, Isaac answers him: "Jim, look at the polls, I've already won." Isaac then turns and walks away. Jim is left standing on the stage, more furious than he has ever been.

After the debate coverage ends, a family in Cincinnati, Ohio is in shock and terribly worried about what they just witnessed. Brian Nolan shuts off the TV, feeling faint, because he is suddenly afraid of the future. He tells his wife, "Oh, Mary, it looks like all we've worked for over the past twenty years is going right out the window!"

Mary is crying over the potential loss of everything they've worked for. She gathers enough composure to stop crying long enough to speak. "I know Brian. I can't believe this, all that struggling for us both to get college degrees, working during the day and going to school at night to be able to afford nice things. This house, our 401(k) and retirement savings, private schools and college funds for the kids to make their lives better, it's all for naught." The more she thinks about Isaac's plans, the sadder she gets, and she starts crying again.

Brian responds with "Unbelievable! Now, we don't know how many others are going to move into this house with us, or if we'll even get to stay here. As for the boys going to Ohio State, who knows what the government will have them do? All those extra math classes to prepare them for engineering were possibly for nothing."

Catching her breath, Mary realizes there may be another solution, but she doesn't like it: "Maybe we should consider leaving the country."

Brian is on the same wavelength and replies, "I'm thinking the same thing, but let's wait until next week to see if the polls don't change. If they don't, I say we take out our 401(k) and get out of the country as soon as possible."

As she thinks about the hopelessness of the political situation, she says, "I don't think we have a choice. How could our country fail us like this? This is unbelievable." She starts crying again before she can even finish her statement.

Brian continues, "My dad has to be turning over in his grave. He gave his life for this country in Iraq, and he taught me the values of America, freedom, and working hard to get ahead." Then he begins tearing up, too, as he thinks about his dad.

At the Cordonia home in Queens, New York, the reaction to the debate is quite different. Eva and her mother are watching the commentary after the debate. After that ends, Eva shuts off the TV. She too is crying, but it is because she is overjoyed at the possibility of a better life. She exclaims, "Mama, this is a miracle from God!" She lifts her hands and looks toward Heaven in praise. Continuing her sentiment, she says, "Soon, we won't have to worry about where our next meal is coming from!"

Eva's mother explains further, "I know, honey. You've not had the life that your father and I envisioned for you when we came here thirty years ago. This was supposed to be the land of opportunity, but it sure hasn't worked out that way!"

Eva goes on to relate more of her sad history: "Since Jose was killed by the gangs three years ago, it's been so hard raising Teresa. I don't know what I would do if not for you. Sixteen dollars an hour, twenty-eight hours a week, just doesn't go very far, and tips are way down."

Eva's mother regains the hope they felt just a few minutes earlier and comforts Eva with, "Don't worry, honey. President Wolfe will take care of us. Soon, we won't have to worry about a roof over our heads, or food, and you can enjoy time with your daughter the way you're supposed to. This really is the greatest country in the world!" They hug each other and cry.

END CHAPTER

CHAPTER THREE

PRE-ELECTION PLANS

OCTOBER 29TH

Houston, Texas is the location of the Taylor/Neilsen Campaign Headquarters. The walls are covered with national, regional, and political maps, as well as campaign posters which say "Elect Taylor/Neilsen in 2036."

The morning after the debate, Jim and his running mate Jacob Neilsen are at their headquarters, sitting at a table drinking coffee, when Jacob brings up the latest polls. Jacob is very discouraged by the state of things and tells Jim, "I've just seen the latest polls after last night's debate. You only had a two percent push! We're still down five percent, and we're losing every one of the toss-up states by almost ten percent. I don't see any way we can win this election. We'll never have enough electoral votes! We may get the popular vote, but the electoral vote will never happen." He sighs and then continues, "It's sad to think about the loss of our great country."

Jim looks at Jacob in horror for Jacob's lack of confidence. "What kind of VP candidate are you, giving up before we've even begun to fight?! Don't give up on the American people, Jacob! The majority of them want to be free, and *they* will vote for us. It's up to us to be freedom's last stand!"

As Jacob hands Jim some papers, he responds with, "Jim, just look at these numbers!"

Jim looks at the numbers and tells Jacob, "This is crazy! How can people fall for this communist agenda?"

Jacob answers, "Well, we do have the most states, but we just don't have the populist Northeast or California. If you ask me, people in this country have been brainwashed since their youth by the school system. This has been building since we were kids. They want to be under a socialist leadership, because they don't understand history and can't see that there *is* a better way."

Jim realizes how dire their situation is, but despite how bad things may seem, Jim continues to use optimism. He tells Jacob, "I've thought that for a long time, too. Let's get back on track, though. We can't let this happen!"

Jacob: "But we do have laws in this nation, and if the people vote to remove the Constitution, then we are powerless to stop it."

Jim's resolve to keep going takes over, and he tells Jacob: "The Northeast and the West Coast are the *only* states voting for this. The majority of states want to be free, and most *people* want to be free. We cannot let this happen, and I vow right now, I *will* not let it!"

Unfortunately, Jim's head-holding, headache-stricken companion Jacob is still doubtful. "What are you going to do? You can't stop them from voting for it."

Jim slams his hands down on the table, scoots back, and gets up so excitedly his chair falls back. He exclaims, "Oh, yes I can! We'll not change, it's that simple. Some people may want to run away from being the United States of America, and Isaac can have his new country if he has to, but all of the states that don't secede will simply remain the United States of America."

Jacob looks up at Jim with fear and gets up slowly. "Are you serious? How, exactly, can we do that, and what do you mean by 'secede'?"

Jim gives Jacob a look of worry over Jacob's disbelief. "I thought you loved your country and were willing to *fight* for it!"

Brightening a little, Jacob asks, "I am, Jim, you *know* that, but how?"

Jim runs over to the giant political map, pointing at it as he goes. "Look, the states that vote against it simply won't switch to this new utopian government when Isaac's states do. Can't you see, we'll just remain the real USA, or what's left of it, the land of the free, the United States of America! I guarantee you the Governor of Georgia Bill Roberts will join us, and I believe most of the other states will. I already planned it out most of the way a long time ago, when Isaac first took office. I've never trusted him, and it's obviously justified. Anyway, we'll make a united stand to not switch over and to not recognize the new laws. We'll let them have their own land, and we'll keep ours. It's that simple!"

Jacob shakes his head, still disbelieving that there's a possibility of saving his beloved country. "I don't think it will work. I just don't believe that people today have enough passion for basically another Civil War."

Jim walks back over to the table and sets his chair upright. He and Jacob sit back down at the table, and Jim grabs a land line phone, which he, like several other governors, have had specially secured against any form of tampering. He starts dialing. "Let's find out. Billy! Yeah, Jim Taylor; how are you?"

Bill, on the other end of the call, is also using one of these special land line phones. He has been looking at a national map as well. "Jim Taylor, I thought you might be calling! You're not going to support this new *government*, are you?"

Jim: "That's what I'm calling about. I'm here in Houston with Jacob at our Campaign Headquarters, and I told him you would be willing to fight with me, if we had to, in opposition to Isaac's new government."

Bill: "Of course, and I've already talked to Jerry and John. Both Alabama and Tennessee are with us. You *bet*, we're not gonna let this happen to *our* states! The Governor of South Carolina's also on board, as soon he gets confirmation that you are."

Jim: "That's great news, Billy – I knew you wouldn't let me down!"

Jacob whispers to Jim, "He said 'yes'?"

Jim moves the phone away from his face just enough to be able to answer Jacob. "Of course he did, Jacob, and he already has a few more governors who are with us. We are *not* going to let these United States fall to a communist government!" Moving the phone back into position so he can talk to Bill, he continues that conversation. "Billy, let's all meet tomorrow morning at the governor's mansion in Austin. Have the other governors you talked to show up as well, and we'll discuss a plan of continuation, that is, to continue to recognize the non-communist USA as our nation. I have a lot of ideas."

Bill: "I'm sure you do! See ya tomorrow morning."

Jim is getting more excited as he ends the conversation. "Great, 8 am. We have a lot to do!"

By the time Jim and Bill hang up, Jacob is returning to life. "Ok, Jim, what's going on?"

Talking with Bill confirmed Jim's thoughts and raised his excitement even further. He answers Jacob, "Well, we have Georgia, Tennessee, Alabama, and South Carolina ready to break off. All the governors are flying to Austin tonight for a meeting at eight o'clock tomorrow morning. We're off to a good start. I don't see any reason we can't have several states ready to split off by next week. Our America will survive. We will not give over to this communist, not today, not next week, not *ever!*"

Rubbing the back of his head out of stress, Jacob starts to gain confidence and tells Jim, "Wow, this doesn't seem possible, but we may just succeed! You're right, I had lost all hope. Thanks for keeping me straight and for always being the great American patriot."

Jim humbly answers, "I'm just doing what needs to be done. Thank all those in history who fought so that we could have these freedoms. We're only continuing the battle against tyranny, and we must not lose!"

That same morning a meeting is held by Isaac and his cabinet at a golf course in California. As they are all standing around talking, Isaac tees off. He hits a shot straight down the fairway. The Secretary of Labor Matthew Roberts is the first to comment, "Good shot, Isaac! You're on top of your game today."

Isaac replies, "Well, I can't let my cabinet members beat me here, now can I?"

Another cabinet member Pablo Martinez chimes in, "Yes, I wouldn't want a riot under my watch."

As the whole golf party is laughing with Pablo, Samantha Jones continues with the joke, "What, you as Secretary of Homeland Security, don't want a riot?"

Pablo retorts, "No more than you would want a mortgage collapse, Samantha my dear, like we saw at the turn of the century. It just wouldn't be good for the Secretary of Housing."

They all continue laughing as Matthew chimes in, "Well, as Secretary of Labor, maybe I should fire you all!"

While Isaac is happy with the camaraderie in his cabinet, he refocuses on the game, thinking to himself, "I'm up five strokes, with only two more holes to go after this one."

Isaac's concentration is then broken by Pablo shouting, "About time for a blow up hole!" They all laugh and continue to play golf. After several more holes and time spent in sand traps, the party is finally at the eighteenth hole and ready to tee off. Pablo, who never can let a good jab opportunity go to waste, puts his arm around Isaac and tells him, "Triple-bogey, Mr. President. You're only two strokes over Matthew."

Matthew cheerfully interjects, "I'm feeling good, too!"

Isaac, ever confident, "I'm well aware of the situation, and, like this election, I have it well under control."

The election then takes over the tone of their conversation, and Samantha announces, "Yes Isaac, I was just talking to your campaign manager this morning. You have 277 electoral votes, guaranteed. It looks like you will soon be our first Czar!"

Matthew, following form, realizes the gravity of their situation. "We're going to have a lot to do once this election is over. The transition from capitalism to socialism is not going be easy. We'll have 170 million workers who will make the same amount of money. That's the *easy* part. Assigning everyone a new job to benefit the Utopian Society will be tricky. The hardest part will be making them all happy!"

Samantha is feeling the weight of her position, too. "Well, what about *me*? Trying to give everyone just 250 square feet to live in won't be easy. Those rich capitalists are not going to take too kindly to sharing their homes with others, especially the homeless. I'm going to need help from you, Pablo, if we're going to keep order."

Pablo reassures them, "I've been working on that. I figure we're going to have several riots from people who don't see the light and resist the common good."

Isaac adds, "There will be a few rough spots, but it won't be that bad, once everyone sees the benefit of not having any homelessness and starvation due to the inequality of capitalism. It won't be long before ninety-eight percent of the people will agree, and the other two percent will come along soon after that."

Matthew is still not convinced. Shaking his head, he tells them, "I don't know, Isaac. I hope you're right. Take Texas, for example. They're not going to accept it peacefully, and Jim Taylor is probably only going to make it worse."

Pablo nods in agreement and adds, "Taylor is definitely a problem, and I may have to arrest him."

Totally disgusted, Samantha continues with "I agree. Jim is just plain evil!"

Isaac is not about to let anyone jeopardize his dream and tells them, "No, no, no, there is good in everyone. Jim will come around and see the better way!"

Matthew, staring at Isaac, angrily says, "No he won't. He wants power, and he won't be happy when I tell him his new role is a prison guard instead of a governor, especially when he'll have to give up his wealth."

Looking shocked, Pablo exclaims, "Jim Taylor, a prison guard?"

Matthew continues, "Yeah, based on his personality and talents, he will benefit society the most as a security guard. We've already used everyone's school aptitude tests to determine the best occupation for each person, based on their abilities and personality. Next comes job placement."

Isaac tees off and then says, "You really think Jim will be a problem?" The ball goes right down the middle.

Pablo speaks with certainty, "Absolutely, he *will* be trouble!" and then tees off with a beautiful shot, right past Isaac's ball. After the rest of them tee off, they continue their walk to their next shot. Instead of driving golf carts, they decided to walk the eighteen holes, as this is better for the environment.

Isaac, starting to wonder if his cabinet is right about Jim Taylor, asks "So, Pablo, what do you advise we do with Jim to keep him from inciting riots?"

Pablo answers, "I don't know, Isaac. That's a tough one. If we put him in jail, he'll become a martyr, which will only make things worse. If we do nothing, he's sure to lead riots."

Matthew thinks it over for a moment before he replies, "Well, since we all know he's power hungry, how about, we offer him a powerful position in the socialist government? When he joins, the rest will follow him."

Isaac is very happy with Matthew's response, "Great idea, a perfect diplomatic solution! We offer him the lead of the Southern Region, where we expect the most resistance. He'll calm everyone down, and the transition will go much smoother. It will be better for all. You guys are a great set of advisors! See? Diplomacy always wins out!" Then he hits his next shot, and the ball lands right on the green by the flag. "Looks like I'll birdie this hole! I told you guys, I have this under control, just like the election. I'm going to call Jim right now." Isaac pulls out a cell phone and dials. "Jim, this is Isaac."

When Isaac calls, Jim is in his campaign office in Houston, marking a national map. (Some states are labeled "F" for "Free," and some others are labeled "CL" for "Capture state capital and then Liberate." Others are marked "U" for "Utopian.") He has dedicated a special phone to Isaac so that he *knows* when Isaac is calling. "Hello, Isaac. Are you calling to concede the election?"

Isaac chuckles and says, "We both know I've won. The people have won! The Utopian Society is inevitable and is on its way."

"Hmm, is that so?" Jim then continues writing "CL" on the state of New Mexico on the map. "We'll see. It's a very close electoral map."

Isaac ignores Jim's comment as he goes on to say, "Yes, but I have 277 guaranteed votes, and you know it. Your pollsters know it. Everyone knows it, which is the reason for this call. I consider you a valuable member of society, with lots of influence on the common person. You can help lead this revolutionary and perfect Utopian Society. You can mark your place in history! I'm offering you the lead of the Southern Region. You will report only to me, as one of my four Regional Leaders, with many people reporting to you. What do you think?"

Jim continues looking at his map and replies, "Well, I have been eyeing the South, and I do want to make my mark in history."

Isaac enthusiastically answers, "Great! Then, I take that as a 'Yes'?"

"But," Jim responds, "What if, by some miracle, I win? Say, Wisconsin has a major snow storm, and only a few people get out and vote, and the state goes to me? It could put me in the winner's seat in that case. How about you come and work for me? I've been thinking, after analyzing the debates, that you have some great ideas. There should be no homeless or starving kids in America. It's a travesty. I will want you on my cabinet, in the new role, Secretary of Human Rights in America."

Ecstatic with Jim's answer, Isaac tells him, "Jim, I am so happy to hear you talk like that! I can see you're starting to come around. If, by some miracle, you do win, it would be my honor to be the first Secretary of Human Rights."

"Great, it's a deal then!"

"Yes," Isaac continues, "Let's agree to be at the Obama Hotel in Washington, DC for the election results. Once the winner is declared, you can join me on the podium, and we can give a joint speech."

Jim, continuing to show hope, "Or, you can join me when I win."

Isaac enthusiastically answers, "Exactly, agreed?"

Jim adds, "Yes, but the winner should have time alone first, to shine in the moment and give his victory speech. Then, the conceding party can give his speech shortly thereafter."

The ever-confident Isaac responds, "That's a good idea. Let the people enjoy their moment with the newly elected Czar."

Jim chimes in with, "or President!"

Isaac, wishing to wrap up the conversation, "Yes, of course, my staff will be in touch with your staff to make the necessary arrangements."

Jim: "Great, I look forward to the results next week."

Isaac concludes his side of the conversation with, "Thanks Jim, see you election night. We'll plan on having dinner at, say 5, before some of the polls start closing at 6."

"Perfect, see you then," and Jim hangs up.

Isaac, feeling quite satisfied with how his phone call went, tells his golf party, "See guys, Jim's coming around. He's agreed to lead the Southern Region under me and will give a concession speech shortly after I've been declared the winner of this election."

As Isaac sinks his putt, Pablo tells him, "I gotta hand it to ya, Isaac. It looks like you really do have this under control."

Back at the Taylor/Neilsen headquarters, Jim continues to work on his election map. Jacob, always the pessimist, asks Jim, "You're not really going to offer Isaac a job in our administration, are you?"

Jim fires back at him, "If, somehow we win, I *definitely* will! He'll help bring the country together, and we need to address issues like homelessness and starvation. People just don't help each other like they used to before FDR. They learned to depend upon the government to get them out of trouble, and family members grew away from each other. I want to restore America, not with government programs, but people's attitudes. Isaac may be the perfect person for that job."

"Maybe," Jacob continues, "but if we lose, what about this position in the South you said you would take? Are you giving up on the split?"

Jim looks at Jacob with a hurt expression and says, "Don't you know me better by now? I was bluffing then."

Jacob: "You, dishonest? That's not like you."

A very determined Jim retorts with fire in his eyes, "This is war! I said I was eyeing the South, and I agreed to go to dinner with him and give a speech shortly after the election results come in. I left out what kind of speech it would be, but I *am* eyeing the South!

Jacob smiles and says, "You are right about that. This *is* war – guess you spun that conversation around!" as he gently hits Jim's arm with rolled up papers.

They both walk over to the table and sit down. Jim continues talking, more calmly now, "The best part is, now we have time, and Isaac doesn't suspect a thing, because he lives in his ivory tower world and is oblivious to our plans, much like the Democrats were in 2030 when Iran nuked London. They said that nobody would ever do anything like that. It never crossed their minds. They thought Iran was only using the technology for energy and had no clue how the world works, how everyone just wants to kill everyone. You can't bury your head in the sand and pretend everyone is peaceful. It has never been that way, starting with Cain and Abel, which this generation doesn't even know about."

"We humans can be an evil race, that's for sure, and with domination on our minds," Jacob quietly says.

Jim begins to show his excitement again and replies, "Exactly, and this is why it is our duty to fight for freedom, every single one of us! We are going to do this, and we're going to make it work. The world is depending on us once again!"

OCTOBER 30TH

The next morning at eight o'clock, at the Taylor/Neilsen Houston Headquarters, Jacob and three guests are gathered at the entrance. They all walk in and sit down at a long conference table. Jim is standing at the end of the table; behind him is a large American flag. Jim gently bangs his hand on the table to get everyone's attention and starts the meeting. "First, I want to thank everyone for coming here on such short notice. America is in grave danger once again, and the future of the Free World depends on what we do here this morning. The weight is heavy, but I know that by the grace of God and through our hard work, it can be done. We can keep freedom alive! We have five states represented here today, and we know that twenty-two other states are going to vote against Isaac and his communistic regime. It is our job to construct a concrete plan so that all of the states which believe in freedom can break off from Isaac's new country at 3:30 am, Eastern Time, right after election night.

Governor John Gordon of Tennessee asks, "Why at 3:30 am? Why not at midnight, or even 11:59 pm? The good, God-fearing people of Tennessee don't want to be socialistic, even for just three and a half hours!"

Jim has had his eyes focused solely on John as John was speaking, but then he turns to show that he wants everyone present to understand him as he answers. "The middle of the night will give us the element of surprise working in our favor. Isaac expects me to give a concession speech around 1 to 2 am, and he'll not suspect a thing until around then. We will have from the time we verify we have lost the election until then to put our plan into action."

Governor Jerry Clanton of Alabama then asks, "What is the plan, as it stands now, and how many blanks do we have to fill in?"

Jim answers, "It's not that complicated, but it will take careful planning if we want to be successful. We will have to secure the borders of all of our states. Indiana will be difficult, but it is crucial in order to claim the Great Lakes as part of the United States to maintain access. We also have to limit riots from those who vote for Isaac. Miami is going to be a *huge* problem, but we'll get to it later. New Mexico is also a problem, and we will need to take that over."

Governor Roberts: "You intend to start a war with New Mexico?"

Jim: "It is strategically located by Texas and Mexico, and we must *not* let it be controlled by Isaac. I plan on taking it over swiftly and without much loss of life."

Governor Clanton asks, "While we're on that particular subject, what *are* we going to do about a military?"

"Well, Jerry," continues Jim, "I've already talked to leading officials at the Pentagon regarding the Army, Navy, Air & Space Forces, and Marines. As you know, they are all former generals or admirals, and they are loyal to the cause of freedom and to the United States. They are behind *us* one hundred percent."

Governor Roberts: "What about the Coast Guard?"

Jim answers him directly, "The Coast Guard is under Pablo's control, so I'm leaving them out of this conversation, but with the support of the five major military branches, we are in really good shape."

Jim then addresses the whole room: "Also, General Maghee revived the MX missile system that has been in its storage bin in Utah. This will give us control over a large percentage of the U.S.'s nuclear arsenal, which will give us good footing, not just against Isaac, but against China, Russia, and everyone else as well. We also control the nuclear defense shield satellite right here in Houston. Sadly, there is a back up satellite controlled from California, so the Utopians will have one of those as well."

He pauses briefly for a sip of water before continuing. "General Maghee also has put a plan into place to conduct war games for the next two weeks, with all troops on call, so that they may be used in an operation. I'm sure you've seen the reports supposedly leaked out of China about their wanting to take over Taiwan, once and for all. This unrest is the perfect excuse to have a majority of platoons ready to be deployed. What they don't know is that they will be deployed to the United States to work with the National Guard to keep riots at a minimum, protect our borders, and to take back New Mexico."

Governor Roberts asks, "So you leaked false information about China wanting to take over Taiwan?"

Jim: "No, they *want* to. The report isn't even false, and it works out perfectly for us. We will have the military on call election night, and Isaac will have no answer to it, which will increase our chances of success dramatically. The Utopians will not be able to fight, not that Isaac would anyway."

Governor Gordon then asks, "But, what if someone in the army gets wise and tips off Isaac? I think this is too great of a risk."

Jim: "Yes, there is a slight risk, but it's a calculated one. The Army is mainly on our side. These people are out there fighting for our freedom, and the only one who knows what's really going on is General Maghee. The rest are just following orders."

Jacob enthusiastically adds, "It's a great plan! I think this may actually work!" A shocked Jim quickly shoots him a scornful look and then regains his composure.

Governor Clanton then asks, "But how do we get the other twenty-two states involved? Once again, the more people who know, the higher the odds Isaac will be tipped off."

Jim takes a breath and lets out a long sigh. Then, he answers his friend and addresses the table: "That is true, but we must secure the capital of each state. Out of the twenty-two remaining states, there are four states with Democratic governors: Colorado, Iowa, Florida, and North Carolina. For the other eighteen states, I know that we can only really count on Indiana, Kentucky, Oklahoma, Louisiana, Mississippi, and Alaska, which gives us a starting base of eleven states. It would be nice to have all twenty-seven, but Jerry, you are absolutely right. We need to understand that the more people who are in on this plan, the greater the chance of something going wrong. We should unite these eleven states and make our break at 3:30 am. Once people see how successful this is, they will gladly join us. I will personally go visit each of the remaining six governors over the weekend and solidify our plans. The eleven of us can all meet here Monday morning to finalize things to make it an airtight plan."

Governor Clanton asks, "What about Virginia? Jacob, isn't your Commonwealth going to remain loyal to the U.S.?"

Jacob starts, "Well…" as Jim verbally shields him, interrupting by getting up and going to the US map on west wall.

"Look," Jim says, "Virginia is suffocated by North Carolina, Maryland, and West Virginia, plus polls show us only winning by five percent there. It's too dangerous for them at this time without mass rioting. We will get Virginia soon after we take over New Mexico and show our resolve and our military might. I'm sure the good people of those three states will all demand they be returned at once."

"I'm not so sure," adds Governor Roberts. "I think we'd want to have as many as possible on board right away."

Jim answers, "Monday, when General Maghee and all eleven Governors are present, we'll discuss that and the detailed plans of annexing New Mexico, as well as the plan to take care of Miami."

Governor Clanton suspiciously questions, *"Take care* of Miami?"

Jim responds, "We'll talk about it Monday when everyone's here. It's not a good solution, but I'm afraid it may be the *only* solution."

Governor Gordon then asks, as if to want to wrap things up, "So what do we do until Monday?"

Jim concludes by saying, "Start working with your National Guard and police forces to prepare for social unrest after the election, but do *not* tip them off! Just let them know that whichever way the election goes, there are going to be protests and violence, and remind them that they need to be ready. Find your loyal leaders, and be prepared to let them in on what is going on election night. We cannot fail, because if we do, everything our ancestors and loved ones have ever suffered in the name of freedom has been for naught. They will have fought and died for nothing. We cannot let that happen. They must be vindicated and their memories must be upheld. Freedom *must* ring!"

NOVEMBER 1ST

In the bowling center which is located in the White House basement under the North Portico, Isaac and some of his cabinet members have gathered for a Saturday morning meeting while bowling a series of three games. Isaac is on one knee after making a shot, and he moves his arm down in triumph for his strike, with a shout of "Yes!" before getting up.

Pablo high-fives him, saying, "Nice shot, soon-to-be Czar!"

A smiling Isaac, says, "Thank you, it feels like I'm on a roll!" before sitting down.

As she gets up to take her shot, Samantha chimes in, "That's six in a row, now. You're half-way to 300."

A relaxed Matthew, with his arms outstretched along the back of the couch, asks, "How often do you come down here to bowl?"

Isaac: "Remember, before I became President, I bowled in a weekly league. I still like to come down here to practice whenever I can. I think Richard Nixon did a good thing when he had the White House bowling center built."

Pablo chuckles lightly as he says, "Ah, yes, good ole Tricky Dick, the only President to resign before impeachment."

Isaac sighs before saying, "True, he was a man with many faults, but we must never forget what he accomplished in 1972. What he did with China was astounding!"

Matthew: "That's right. 'Only Nixon can go to China!'"

After finishing her turn, Samantha sits down next to Isaac and says, "Enough about Nixon! Sir, why did you call a Saturday morning meeting, at the bowling center no less?"

Isaac is caught somewhat off-guard by her tone and slowly answers, "Well." He then pauses to grab his water bottle, reaching over his phone, on the nearby coffee table. He takes a drink, although he isn't really thirsty but wanted a reason to pause and collect his thoughts. After a few seconds, he continues, "I wanted a status update. We only have four days, including today, until the election, and I want to make sure we have everything set up. The people will want this transition to go as smoothly as possible. It is our duty to make it happen, with no surprises. They need us to be fully prepared to change over to the new system immediately." He looks over at Matthew and asks, "How are we doing on Labor?"

Matthew suddenly tenses up and sits up straight. "Things are actually going very well, sir. We have everything organized. As you know, I've restructured the US into twelve Districts. Each one has a District Headquarters, and the staff of every District Headquarters has compiled lists of all businesses, even down to the level of children selling lemonade. We will be able to seize control of every single business immediately. Thanks to the IRS and DHS, we have their true financials. In fact, we completely control all companies now, including payrolls. They just don't know it yet. No one will have any more money than anyone else. I've been working with Eric, and he's done a great job of getting the banking industry ready to seize all private funds, so we will control every individual's bank accounts the second you become Czar."

Isaac claps before saying with excitement, "Excellent, you've done some very good work in a short time!" He then turns to Samantha and asks, "What about Housing? Has your task force been able to take care of housing, Samantha?"

Samantha: "Well, sir, I've followed Matthew's District strategy, and we've managed to account for every single person. By taking all the land and existing buildings and rearranging things, each person will have 250 square feet, which will *completely* wipe out homelessness. In fact, by doing this, we'll get rid of the inefficiency of capitalism, which will free up over forty percent of all houses, apartments, and inns, which we can then convert to other government uses."

Isaac: "That's fantastic news, Samantha! Our dream for America to become a Utopian paradise may finally become a reality." A very happy Isaac looks around the room saying, "Keep up the good news, people!" He then turns to Pablo and asks, "Pablo, what do you have for us?"

Pablo looks down in shame while rubbing his neck as he says, "Well, sir, my job is difficult. There are millions of people who don't share our ideas. They are not going to vote for you, and we will be taking their money and homes from them. It's for their good, and the good of all, but they will be angry and defiant. Many won't be willing to give up their extravagant way of life, even if it is for the common good."

A visibly upset Isaac leans towards him and asks, "So, you're not prepared? We only have four days left, Pablo!"

Pablo backs away and continues, "I didn't say that. We are preparing as we speak. You asked, and I'm letting you know the reality of the situation, Isaac. Over the last few days my people have been recording and observing everyone's phone calls, texts and emails, and many of the wealthier citizens are planning on revolting or leaving the country."

Isaac picks up his cell phone and calls the Secretary of the Treasury Eric Masterson. He answers Isaac, "Hello, Mr. President! Can I help you?"

Isaac: "Eric, I hear we have a problem. Many of the rich people are planning on leaving the country! We need to seize control of their money now, before they transfer it into foreign accounts."

With confidence Eric replies, "I anticipated this and actually started working on it two weeks ago. In fact, all monies being sent overseas have been rerouted to a special fund I created. Most of the foreign banks and governments are cooperating, but since some aren't, we've activated the 2030 Foreign Bank Bill to hold these monies for one month, and by the time the month expires you will be Czar, so we will keep the money indefinitely."

Isaac: "Great! So, we *do* control all of their money?"

Eric: "Every penny! ... uh ... sir."

Isaac: "Wonderful, keep up the good work!" He hangs up and turns to Pablo. "Now, Pablo, what do you think we should do about closing down the airlines? How important is it that these people don't leave the country?"

Pablo: "I think we should close down the airlines under some fake terrorist report, using the 2030 Homeland Anti Terrorist Bill."

Matthew: "We need those people here for labor in order to keep everything running. Like it or not, a lot of the rich people are leaders of their companies, and we will need their expertise."

Pablo: "Perfect! Not only will I close the airports, but I'll close all of our borders under the Anti Terrorist Bill."

Samantha: "Wait a minute, guys, if we do all this, Americans may start to revolt now and decide to vote for the other party on Tuesday."

Matthew: "Good point, if we close everything down, Jim will seize the opportunity to twist the minds of the American public against us and rally enough of them to overcome the poll deficit."

Isaac: "We can't have people leaving. This is for their own good. One day they will all understand that."

Pablo: "That's the beauty of the 2030 Homeland Anti Terrorist Bill. We just leak a rumor from Iran that terrorists claim to have perfected the dirty nuke, and we close down all borders and air space. No one will suspect a thing. We'll have all the media outlets report this and have everyone fearing for their lives. They'll all rally behind you, Isaac, thinking how presidential you look, taking control of the situation and making sure everyone is safe."

Isaac: "I love this idea – good work, Pablo! All three of you have done well. I know we're being a little dishonest here, but we have to protect the American people, even those who are naive and ignorant, who don't yet understand the way. We need to be proactive, and a little deception to make Utopia achievable for all is worth it."

Pablo: "Thank you, sir, I'll fabricate and leak that message right away."

Isaac: "Hey Pablo, wait. I have another idea. Why don't I give a speech tonight and let that be the first the American people hear of this imminent threat? Instead of telling the media about the threat, tell them I will be giving an emergency speech about a threat to Homeland Security. Have them be ready to stop everything for my live speech at 8 pm Eastern. Let them know this is a serious event and that Americans are in jeopardy."

Pablo: "Great idea, sir!"

Isaac smiles and says, "Thank you! OK, you all have more work to do, and you know how important it is to the country. Keep up the good work, and be back at the Oval Office for my speech tonight. Pablo, I will be calling you this afternoon to go over the details." Now that the meeting has concluded, everyone leaves except for Isaac, who stays and finishes his game, bowling a perfect 300.

That evening, Jim and Jacob are relaxing at their headquarters, after a long week of planning. They are sitting on a couch watching TV, with popcorn and beer, getting ready to enjoy a football game, when Jacob tells Jim, "Glad we could take time off the campaign to watch this game."

Jim replies, "How could we miss this, Texas versus Virginia Tech? My alma mater is going to win this game for sure!"

Jacob excitedly says, "We'll see – you might be ten-point favorites, but our quarterback is streaky."

The TV shows the kickoff, and all of a sudden an announcer breaks in. "We now interrupt the game in progress for an emergency speech by President Wolfe."

A very annoyed Jim whines, "What is he up to now? This can't be any good."

The announcer states matter-of-factly, "And now, the President of United States, Isaac Wolfe."

Isaac is shown at the presidential podium, with various flags behind him, as he begins his speech:

>"My fellow Americans, I have received very troubling news. Terrorists continue to work against us, despite the best efforts of our government over the past ten years to reach a diplomatic solution. We now have confirmation that a terrorist cell in Iran has developed the dirty nuke. We have been afraid of this day for many years. What this essentially means is that a terrorist can now destroy an entire city with a nuclear bomb that fits inside a brief case. One person with one brief case can sneak into our country and cause the death of millions of Americans. As a result, we are now enacting

the 2030 Homeland Anti Terrorist Bill. As we speak, all airports and borders to Canada and Mexico are being closed in order to ensure that none of these dirty bombs will enter our country, thus ensuring the safety of all who are on American soil against this great threat. We are not going to let these terrorists' threats destroy us. Instead, we will defeat this threat, as we have so many others. We will unite as Americans and, once again, come out victorious.

"Knowing that this threat was possible, we have been working day and night for the past two years, developing a wireless dirty nuke detector. This device will alert us of any dirty bomb within three hundred miles of the device. We are installing these devices in every metropolitan area as we speak. These detectors should be installed within a week, and we anticipate restoring normal travel within a month. We are doing everything we can to protect America and all of you. I appreciate your support in this extreme emergency and know that each and every one of you will fully support and help protect America.

"Thank you for your patriotism. Good night, and rest assured that we are safe. We will not let you down. Thank you."

Isaac walks off, and the game resumes. Jim slams his hand down on the table in front of him, yelling, "I can't believe Isaac just did that! Patriotism? He knows *nothing* about patriotism; he's trying to *destroy* this country!" He takes a deep breath and exhales hard. "I don't believe his story is true. I haven't heard *anything* about this."

Jacob nods, "Neither have I. I've been wondering how he would keep people from leaving the country. This would fit that purpose perfectly."

Jim continues, "You may be onto something, Jacob. I think he is making this up in order to close the borders to keep people from leaving before the election. He's using this dirty bomb story to make himself look like a savior to America to make sure the people reelect him!"

Jacob agrees, "Yep, this had a dual purpose, alright. We need evidence that it's a false report."

Jim says to Jacob, "I'm going to get that right now! I'm calling Maghee," as he picks up his phone. All he gets, however, is a busy signal. "Busy? Why is he not answering me?!"

Jacob sheepishly answers, "Maybe the threat *is* real and he is on the phone with his advisors."

Jim immediately fires back, "No, it's not real, I guarantee it's not! This is strictly a chess move on Isaac's part to seize control of all the transportation into and out of the country. He will not get away with this!" He starts drumming the table with one hand while he keeps calling with the other. "C'mon, answer me, Maghee, answer me!" Maghee finally answers one of his calls.

A rather annoyed general answers, "Jim?"

A relieved Jim says, "Finally! I've been trying to reach you for the past five minutes, Maghee. What's going on here?!"

General Maghee tells him, "I was on the phone with Pablo Martinez. You using the scrambler?"

"Of course – I don't want Isaac hearing any of this conversation! What's going on?"

General Maghee tells Jim exactly what he suspected. "Well, Martinez is insisting that there is real threat out there, but I know there is not. He would not quite admit in so many words that it was faked, but I got the gist of it. This is simply an election ploy. Dirty nukes are still years away, and besides, we already have those wireless devices deployed everywhere. It's a Class 3-A security clearance item, so only a tiny handful of people know about them. The truth is, we have had them in place for years. We have nothing to worry about."

"Exactly what I thought, Wolfe will stop at nothing to push his communist agenda down America's throat!"

"I agree," Maghee says, "but I need to do a few things for Martinez so he doesn't get suspicious. See you Monday."

"Ok, thanks, see you then," Jim says before hanging up his phone. He then turns to Jacob and starts shouting, "Can you believe this, Jacob?! Isaac has made this whole thing up. He has Americans all in a panic, just so he can be elected and keep people from leaving the country!"

Jacob: "Mmm-hmm, I understand that Jim, but try to calm down. We need to turn this around and make it advantageous to us. There has to be *something* we can do to use this to our advantage."

"You know, you're right," says a much happier, excited Jim. "Once the other governors hear that this is indeed a false report, they will be even more energized to revolt. This will become a rallying cry."

Jacob: "So, Isaac just helped us!"

Jim happily responds, "Yes he did! He shot himself in the foot. True Americans are going to be more passionate now, just like we were when we rallied from Pearl Harbor and 9/11. This is the same thing, an act of war against the American people, only this is worse. It's is an internal attack by our very own President! People should be fueled and willing to fight to the death to oppose this oppressive communistic government. Thank you, Isaac Wolfe, for assuring the United States' victory!"

Jim and Jacob start watching the game again, popcorn and beers in hand. About ten minutes later, Isaac calls Jim. Jim answers, "President Wolfe? What is going on?"

Isaac: "President Wolfe? …Uh…We have a real threat here, Jim. I'm calling all the governors one by one, but I wanted to call you first. Everyone needs to be on high alert for these dirty nukes."

Jim: "Thanks for calling, Isaac. I was planning on calling you. As Governor of a border state to Mexico, I'm very concerned that the terrorists may come across our borders through Mexico. I need those devices now!"

Isaac: "Yes, Jim, all Border States are first in line, but you've got to understand that this will take time."

Jim: "I need to be the first of the first. Remember, we have several highly populated cities and will very likely be a target, right after New York, Chicago and LA."

Isaac continues, "Yes, I understand that, Jim. The Secretary of Defense will have his people contact you shortly, and we will have these devices set up in your state by the end of the night."

"That's great news! What can I do help?" Jim asks with a grin.

Issac: "If I think of anything, I'll let you know. I appreciate your help and support in this matter and look forward to you being my Southern Region Leader after Tuesday's election. I'm glad we already have a unified spirit for the good of the country, Jim."

Jim replies with an even bigger smile on his face, "Well, I look forward to having you retire to my cabinet, but the most important thing is that we must not let one dirty nuke detonate in our country."

Isaac: "Yes, that is the most important thing. See you Tuesday for dinner. We can discuss any other topics then."

"Ok, Isaac, see you then. Don't hesitate to call if you need help," Jim says as he hangs up the phone.

Jacob sets his beer down and claps, saying "Bravo! *That* was a *masterful* performance! You were as cool as can be. You gave no indication that you didn't believe his story."

"Thanks," and then Jim continues, "It's important to keep Isaac completely clueless. If he thinks we're onboard, he will never suspect our plans. I really believe this is going to work. I can feel it!"

Jacob shakes his head and mutters, "It has to work."

Jim fires back, "You bet your bottom dollar, it does! Now, can we get back to the game?"

As Jim is making phone calls, the Nolan family is at an airport in Cincinnati on a plane, waiting to fly to Italy. Mary is sitting in the window seat, and her husband Brian is sitting next to her on the aisle, on the right side of the plane. Their two sons are seated across the aisle. Mary looks out the window and a few seconds later says, "It's hard to believe that in fifteen minutes we're taking off to Modena, Italy to start a new life."

Brian: "I can't believe how well it worked out that my company was able to transfer me this fast to the Modena plant. I pulled a few strings, and here we are. We can start house hunting tomorrow, and I'll start working there next week."

"I'm really worried. Why couldn't we take money out of our 401(k), Mary asks while turning to face Brian.

Brian looks around to make sure no one is listening, then leans over and whispers in Mary's ear, "I think that money has been frozen by the government."

Mary whispers back, "But yet, we were able to empty all twelve thousand from our savings account. It just doesn't make any sense. How were we able to carry all that cash right through security at the airport in a briefcase? This whole thing just feels off to me, Brian."

Brian, "I know Mary, I know, but I don't think we have any other options, do you?"

Their younger child Rick, unaware that they are speaking, loudly asks, "Hey Dad, do you think there will be a high school baseball team for me to play on?"

Brian takes a second to compose himself before turning to the kids. He answers saying, "Sure, Rick... Remember, we will be looking at high schools tomorrow, too. I'm sure one of them will have a baseball team for you to join."

Their elder son George, who's slouching in his chair twiddling his thumbs, asks with irritation, "Have you thought about where I can go to go to college? I'm a senior; I've already worked through and gotten A's in most of my first semester classes. I was supposed to start at Ohio State next fall!"

Brian: "I know, George. I did some research last night, and Italy's top engineering school is only thirty miles from my plant. With your test scores, you're a shoe-in to get accepted."

George: "I don't know, Dad. Man! This is all happening too fast."

Brian: "Stop worrying, George. I'm sure you'll make plenty of new friends, and at some point maybe even a new girlfriend. We'll make a good life for ourselves there, you'll see."

Mary: "And don't forget what Grandma Mae used to say, Honey, 'Where one door slams shut in your face, another one just opened, you just gotta find it.'"

As she finishes speaking, an announcement is made over the loudspeaker. "Attention everyone, we have just been informed that our flight has been cancelled. Everyone must exit the plane. More details will be given at the boarding area, once you're off the plane. This is not an immediate emergency, so do not panic, but please exit the plane in an orderly manner as soon as you can."

People in the plane issue a loud grown. Some begin shouting, as they are mad; others are confused, but most are scared. People gradually get up to grab their things and exit. Brian looks to Mary and whispers, "I bet Wolfe is stopping people from leaving the country. Now we're going to be stuck here!"

Mary: "We don't know that yet. Maybe there is simply a problem with the plane."

Brian: "I hope that's the case, but whatever it is, we'll find out in a few minutes." The family members get up, grab their things from the overhead compartments, and exit the plane, heading to the boarding gate area to stand around and wait for answers with the rest of the passengers.

After several minutes an airline employee goes to the desk and starts speaking over the intercom, saying, "Everyone, may I have your attention, please? President Wolfe has just enacted the 2030 Anti Terrorist Bill. No traffic is to come into or leave the country. All borders are now closed as a security precaution. Please do not panic. He said this is just a precaution to keep us all safe."

Brian says to his family, "I can't believe this! They've trapped us in here, with no way out! It's like a bad nightmare. Don't we have laws and a Constitution to protect us from this? How could this happen?"

Patting his arm, Mary says, "We'll get through this. I don't know how, but we will."

November 3rd

Monday morning, the day before the election, in the Austin governor's mansion, Jim, Jacob, and General Maghee are in a conference room, just to the right of the front door. They are waiting for the other governors to arrive. These will include:

Representing Alabama, Jerry Clanton

Representing Alaska, Mike Sherman

Representing Georgia, Bill Roberts

Representing Indiana, Zach Schwartz

Representing Kentucky, Greg Boone

Representing Louisiana, Bob Cannon

Representing Mississippi, Carey Rhodes

Representing Oklahoma, Victor Mandrell

Representing South Carolina, Sam Wilkerson

Representing Tennessee, John Gordon

Before long the governors come into the building as a group. Jim walks out of the conference room and stands just outside the door with his hands behind his back. He greets them saying, "I would like to personally thank each and every one of you for having the courage to come here this morning and make the tough decisions that are necessary for the survival of the Free World."

Hurriedly, Governor Roberts says as he walks toward the conference room door, "Well, let's get right to it, we don't have much time! What are the plans you have so far?"

Jim puts his hand out to block the door and then says, "Wait a minute, this location isn't secure enough. We need to take a little field trip." He starts walking down a hallway saying, "Follow me." Everyone is looking around puzzled as they follow him.

Jacob runs up to Jim and asks, "Where are we going, Jim?"

Jim keeps walking, saying, "Just keep following me, please." They walk down to the end of the hall and get on a large elevator.

Governor Roberts: "We're going to the top floor?"

Jim: "We are going somewhere; hang on, everyone!" He smiles at the group, then looks down to a keypad and pushes buttons. The elevator starts descending at what seems to be an incredibly fast pace. Everyone but Jim and General Maghee look panicked. The elevator comes to a sudden stop, and the door opens. Jim then says, "We're half-way there! He whispers, "Please follow me and keep quiet for now."

The group gets off the elevator and walks down a hallway. There are metal fire-doors on both sides of the hall. When they reach the thirteenth row of doors Jim stops, goes to the door on the right, and puts his hand up to a hand reader on the wall outside the door. The door opens into a huge windowless conference room. The room has blue wallpaper with red and white trim. There is a large wooden conference table with the image of a bald eagle carved into it. On the far wall is a painting of George Washington. Governor Roberts looks around for a moment, puts his hand on the table and asks, "How far have you taken us?"

Jim: "Oh, we're not there yet." Everyone is puzzled as Jim goes to the painting, removes it to uncover a keypad, and types in a long combination. A hand print reader comes out of the wall. When Jim puts his hand on it, the hand reader goes back into the wall, along with the keypad, and the entire wall starts to lower. In a few seconds it is gone, resting on the floor below. Ahead of them now is a dirt room with a train track and a cart big enough to fit them all. A few feet from the cart, there is a place where wood is stacked.

Jacob: "What the heck is this?!"

Jim: "Everyone, please take a seat." While they're getting in Jim walks to the wood. He moves the wood pile and digs through a thin layer of dirt with his hands, unearthing the door of a safe which contains gas masks. He opens it and grabs a bunch of masks, then walks back to the cart. Once there, he says to the group, "Put these on if you value your lives, then hold on tight!" He gives one to each of them, and gets in the cart.

Jacob takes a mask, looks at it, and says, "What!?"

Jim: "You will need these in about five minutes. There are oxygen tanks underneath the seats. If you look around, you'll find a tube coming from your tank. Plug the tube into your mask so you can breathe." Once everyone has oxygen, Jim pulls a lever and they take off. As they take off, the wall behind them raises back to its original position, closing the exit.

The cart descends, and after about a minute of travel, they are in pitch darkness and continuing to go down. The cart speeds up, rattling and whirring. Once they get to the lowest elevation of the track, a green glowing gas creeps all around them. The governors look around with fear and uneasiness. After several more minutes of traveling, they get past the gas and see lights. They are greeted with a building encased in rock that has a large hanger-style door in front of it that opens. The cart goes inside and comes to a halt. Then the hanger door shuts behind them. Inside it is a garage-like room with a metal door on the far wall. Jim jumps out, taking off his gas mask. Then, he yells so that people can hear him, "You can take your masks off now. We've made it, we're here!"

Governor Sherman of Alaska looks around and asks, "Where is *here*?"

Jim: "We're 24.8 miles underground, about fifty feet away from the Earth's upper mantle.

A concerned Governor Sherman yells, "What?! Our bases don't dare go past ten miles underground. Are you sure this is safe?"

Jim looks over at General Maghee as he says, "It's been here for two years now. I had it built when it began to look like President Wolfe was going to try and switch the country completely to socialism. We needed a top secret hide out, where no cell phones, satellite, or any other forms of technical communication would work. Down here we're completely untraceable, so we can talk here in complete freedom."

Governor Sherman stares at Jim as he says, "Don't you think this is a bit excessive? I mean, c'mon, a secret code on the elevator to go down to a secret room that takes you to another secret room that takes you twenty-five miles below the ground?"

"I like it. You can't ever be too careful," General Maghee says as he looks around the room.

Governor Sherman: "The mantle is five hundred degrees! I ask again, are you sure this is safe?"

Jim: "Yes, the building is covered with heat shields. The heat provides us all the energy we need, and we can use the oxygen from the molten layer. So, yes, it works perfectly." Jim walks to the door and then continues, "There's a conference room this way. We'd be more comfortable there." He opens the door; on the other side of it is a hallway with many doors. He goes to and opens the first door on the left. It's about five feet away from the hall entrance. Inside is a conference room. The room floor is made up of large, glossy, gray tiles. There is a large black table in the middle of the room. On the far wall is a large touch screen. "Now, everyone have a seat, and let's start working on plans to keep freedom alive. We have less than forty-eight hours before we need to secede, and there is a lot we have to cover. At nine o'clock tomorrow night I will escape from the Barack Obama Hotel in disguise, take the governor's plane back to my office in Austin, and use a secret tunnel entry from the north side. From there, I will be in communication with General Maghee, as he is securing all ten of our states with military deployment of the troops that were training to go to Taiwan. We will have the borders of all ten of our states completely guarded with fighter jets and tanks. Also, the fighter jets will be patrolling the Great Lakes. Any intrusion by the Utopians will be immediately dealt with, as in, we *will* shoot to kill."

Governor Schwartz of Indiana takes a seat and then adds, "We're talking about a civil war here, and when the fighting starts, I'm going to be all alone in Indiana, surrounded by Utopians on all but one side. Who knows what will be coming from Lake Michigan or the Ohio River, not to mention the states of Michigan, Ohio, and Illinois. I will need at least double the troops."

General Maghee pats Governor Schwartz on the shoulder, sits down next to him, and answers, "I've thought about that, and don't worry, you'll have four times the amount of troops and firepower. I'm personally overseeing Indiana's defense!"

Governor Schwartz smiles, "So, how are we doing this then?"

Everyone else sits down, and Jim walks to the end of the table, puts his hands on the table and speaks, looking at his various guests, "First things first, we're taking our stuff back! At 3 am, we will have our secret operatives steal the originals of the Constitution, with the Bill of Rights, and the Declaration of Independence, as well as the Federal Copy of the Magna Carta, the Liberty Bell, and the Statue of Liberty. We'll also add extra armaments to safeguard the gold in Fort Knox. We cannot let these symbols of freedom be destroyed. We will set up the Statue of Liberty in the Gulf of Mexico, right outside of Houston. The Liberty Bell will go to Atlanta, and documents will be protected in our new White House, which will be located in Austin. Jacob is overseeing the special units and has the detailed plans."

Governor Roberts: "Alright, what are we going to do about Florida? My state, Georgia, and Alabama, border Florida. What are your plans for Miami? You have alluded to a secret plan for that region in general. We don't want the Utopians in our Gulf!"

Jim fires back, "Absolutely not!" Then he takes a long, deep breath before continuing, "It is with a heavy heart that I have made a decision about Florida. Most of the people in the state of Florida want to be free, but unfortunately, the heavily populated Miami-Ft Lauderdale region is almost completely Utopian, along with small pockets in Tampa and Orlando. We must not let that 10% of the people who are Utopian destroy the state. It would take several generations to change their way of thinking. And *that* is time we simply do not have. They must be shipped into Utopian territory or eliminated. We cannot, and will not, allow communism to exist in the United States."

Governor Rhodes of Mississippi gets up shouting, "Are you suggesting we attack Miami, Ft Lauderdale, Tampa, and Orlando?!?"

Jim: "Look, even if we conquer Miami and Ft. Lauderdale, a large percentage of the people that are there now will never want to be free. It has always been *their* culture to be dependent on the government. They vote as far left as any demographic in the nation! It's hopeless."

Governor Roberts: "So, what are you suggesting?"

Jim: "We wipe it clean… nuclear annihilation."

Everyone but General Maghee, shouts, "What???"

Governor Schwartz: "Are you mad?!?"

Jim: "It's the only workable solution that we've been able to find. If you see another option, *please* say it *now!*"

There is a long awkward pause. Governor Rhodes eventually breaks the silence, saying, "We can't just kill millions of people, Jim."

Jim: "We will give them a two-day warning on Wednesday morning that we will nuke the area at noon on Friday. We will give everyone an opportunity to leave. We will have hundreds of cruise ships, military ships, trains, planes, and buses, *plenty* of transportation venues ready to take everyone to New York, and the communists can disperse those people from there. The few people who want to be free, that live in that area, can just go on up a hundred miles. We will get everyone out of there who wants out."

Governor Rhodes sits back down, crosses his arms, and continues, "I'm not so sure this is a good idea."

General Maghee: "Noted! But, it's the *only* way we can see to completely eliminate the Utopians from the region. Again, if anyone here has any other ideas, now's the time."

Jim looks around at everyone, and there is silence. After waiting about a minute, Jim continues, "That's because there is no other solution. This is the only way to keep the Utopians out of the strategic Gulf of Mexico. A nuclear bomb covers only about fifty miles, so two should do and easily keep the majority of Florida away from the fallout. Besides, it will show Isaac we mean business and, at the same time, show the world we have them."

Governor Rhodes sighs and angrily states, "I guess there is really no other way."

"Well, I'll certainly sleep a lot better at night knowing Florida is on our side," says Governor Bill Roberts.

Jim: "Also Bill, I was thinking, the smoothest way to integrate Florida would be for you to annex the top half of it and make Georgia a super state. Utilize martial law in Tampa and Orlando to have all the Utopians shipped out. The southern part won't be usable for many years, and since most of it is already federal land, I was thinking we would just consider the whole thing federal land until we can create a new state there."

Governor Roberts: "I like that idea. Anyone have any objections to that?"

Governor Clanton: "It makes good sense to me, but, uh, not to be childish, but I think Alabama should have the Panhandle."

Governor Roberts: "That's fair. It's on your side of our states' dividing line. Everyone else agree?" Everyone nods in agreement.

Jim: "Excellent! Now that the southeast is settled, we need to discuss another problem area, New Mexico. I'm simply not comfortable with this state being in the Utopian fold. It is way too close to Austin, so I've had General Maghee compile a plan to overtake the Governor's Mansion at four o'clock Wednesday morning. We will control the state's National Guard troops, as well as their police forces, and we will have extra troops on hand to wipe out any Utopian movements in that state. Those people, too, can be escorted to Utopia."

Governor Mandrell of Oklahoma: "I'm all for that, and I think the majority of Oklahomans will be, too. We border them, and they would be one less thing to worry about."

Jim: "We'll put Senator Fitzgerald from New Mexico in place as their new Governor, and that will bring our states to eleven. There will be unrest, since that state is really 55-45 pro-Utopian, but I think most of the population will come around swiftly, once they see how the other states are faring under socialism. We'll make sure anyone who truly wants to leave New Mexico has the opportunity, too. This is going to be a mess, as everyone will realize the freedoms they have given up once they start living under those rules.

Jacob: "I doubt New Mexico will lose many people; Fitzgerald gives such charismatic speeches." He then rubs his right eyebrow as he says, "What else do we need to think about?"

Jim: "I think we covered everything, except my speech, which I will be giving right at 3:30 am on the Republican Network. They're located here in Austin, and I've arranged for them to still be broadcasting that night. At that time, Isaac and the world will know that we have liberated the United States. I don't think Isaac will attack, but we need to be ready."

Maghee: "We'll be ready! I will *not* let the Utopians onto free, American soil. It's not going to happen."

Governor Gordon: "What about their nuclear defense shield?"

Maghee stands up, walks over to Jim and pats him on the shoulder saying, "I got this one, Jim. I've been thinking all week on this! We take our space planes into outer space and obliterate all of their military satellites early Wednesday morning! They will be blind and unable to use radar as well as their laser shield defense."

Governor Rhodes: "You have planes that can go into outer space?"

Maghee: "We've had 'em since 2000, ever since I was an eighteen year-old corporal, my first special assignment."

Governor Roberts: "Should we take out Russia and China's satellites at that time, too?"

Maghee firmly says, "I plan to take out everyone's."

Jacob: "I'm not so sure we should do that. It could start an unprovoked war."

Jim looks directly at Maghee as he says, "I agree with Jacob. Sorry General, America doesn't start wars. We defend freedoms. We know we can take them out, and they will know we can take them out, so I'd like to hold off on this please. It's never been our way to provoke wars."

Governor Roberts: "You are absolutely correct. I just have a feeling that Russia or China will use a US conflict as a sign of weakness and may exploit it by attacking."

Jim: "Well if they do, they will pay the price. I agree that they may very well try to gain a military advantage in the next few weeks, and we need to be ready, just in case."

Maghee: "Ok, but if we get attacked by Russia immediately, don't blame me, I've warned you."

Jim: "Yes, thanks General, but remember, our goal here is freedom and fair treatment of all."

Maghee: "Ok, anything else?"

Governor Rhodes: "I have a concern. What about our money supply? As a new country, we can't continue to use the old dollar system."

Jim: "Good question and we have that covered. I had Maghee work with the CIA to ascertain the value of all bank accounts of everyone in our ten states, plus New Mexico and

Florida. We have a new money supply being produced and we will credit everyone with the exact same value of their current assets. No one will lose anything that they have worked for. Besides that, Isaac said he'd pay off the previous US debt, so we're looking good to revitalize our nation."

Governor Rhodes: "It looks like you thought of everything. Is the new monetary system going to be based upon gold, or world markets like before?"

Jim: "I plan to go back to the gold standard, as we'll have Kentucky and, therefore, Ft. Knox. And, thanks, I *have* had to think of as many things as possible because the future of the Free World actually does depend on what we do here in the next several days. Ok, if there is nothing else, we all know what to do. Let's get out there and save the world!"

END CHAPTER

CHAPTER FOUR

THE ELECTION

It is Election Day, and we are in Washington D.C. at the five-star Barack Obama Hotel, in the hotel's main restaurant. Isaac and Jim are sitting at a table eating a steak dinner. A server pours champagne into their glasses, and Isaac raises his glass to Jim.

Isaac: "A toast, to a better tomorrow!"

Jim responds in kind, raising his glass, "Yes, indeed, to a better tomorrow!" as they gently clink their glasses together.

Isaac: "So Jim, what is your plan to rein in the South?"

Jim: "Are you assuming you've won the election already? Voting polls don't close for at least an hour."

Isaac: "I know your camp has had to have seen the exit polls, Jim. It's over."

Jim: "As I've told you before, we're expecting a 5% bounce on actual votes. People are too afraid of you and your government to admit to voting for me."

Isaac, insulted by Jim's comment, slips far back into his chair, distancing himself from Jim. "That's ludicrous, Jim! We're not violent. We're a peaceful government."

Jim: "It's like the Carter-Reagan election in 1980. Everyone thought it would be too close to call. Everyone was afraid of being admonished for saying they voted for Reagan, but he won by a landslide."

Isaac: "That was a long time ago, fifty-six years. Things are much different now."

Jim: "Are they? My people tell me I'm going to win. So, what are your plans as the first Secretary of Human Rights?"

Isaac picks up his champagne glass, looks into it, sighs, and takes a drink. "I see you're not giving in yet, so," stretching his hand and bowing slightly "ok, Jim. Let's discuss, hypothetically, what you will do if you lose. Then I will discuss, hypothetically, what I will do if I lose."

Jim: "Well, Isaac, if you were to win, and I became the Leader of the Southern Region, I would do everything in my power to keep peace and promote the *current government*, for the good of the people. I love this country way too much."

Isaac: "That's good to hear. I expect a great speech out of you later tonight."

Jim: "I think you'll be surprised when you hear the speech I have a prepared. It will be very patriotic. What about you?"

Isaac: "If I were to lose and become your Secretary of Human Rights, I would work day and night to fight the injustices of the poor and homeless and to find solutions to give them the basic necessities of life."

Jim nods his head in approval, "I like that, because it's not right that people in this country are homeless or starving. I hope your new cabinet position will be able to unify Americans in helping the poor, out of their free will."

An uncomfortable Isaac shifts in his chair. "Jim, Jim, let's be realistic here. You are not winning this election."

Jim: "I thought we were talking hypothetically."

Isaac: "In seven hours it will be midnight. I will be giving my acceptance speech as the new Czar of a new nation. Shortly after that, you will be giving your speech as the leader of the Southern region. I think it would be a good idea to go over some details for your new job."

Jim: "Remember 1980, Isaac. It's not over until all the votes are counted, and besides, if you did win, what are you really going to do with a socialistic state? For example, what about your steak dinner and upscale restaurants like this, movie theaters, bowling alleys, and other entertainment places for people to relax and unwind after a hard day's work?"

Isaac: "Well, Jim, my plan is equality for all! Right now, many people want to have these luxuries, but they can't afford them. It's not fair that some can have them while others can't. These things will exist, but in a state where all will have the opportunity. People will put their names on a list, and when their turn comes, they will be able to eat a nice dinner, go bowling, or indulge in the activity of their choosing."

Jim: "What?! You want people to put their name on a list and wait months, possibly years, to go eat a nice steak dinner?"

Isaac takes a sip of champagne, "This ensures equality for all."

Jim: "So, what about you? I'd like to see you wait for months to eat here."

Isaac: "Well, this hotel will be reserved for the government."

Jim: "I thought you said equality for all, but equality apparently stops here!"

Isaac: "People need a leader, Jim, someone to admire and to look up to. Look at the history of the world, kings, queens, pharaohs. From the beginning of time, people have needed a leader."

Jim: "So it's your duty to the American people to eat steak every night while everyone else is waiting months for *one* opportunity?"

Isaac: "Yes, I need to be a source of inspiration to my people. They need to see their leader in a position of power."

Jim: "You're taking away freedoms!"

Isaac: "Freedom? Is that what you call your belief system?"

Jim: "Yes, freedom to choose. You want to be a pizza delivery man? You can do that. You want to go to college and better your life? You can do that. Look at me. I cleaned stables at the rodeo, working twelve hours a day while searching for oil veins. I was free to do that, and look at me today."

Isaac: "You're not free; you're a slave to Capitalism! Correct me if I'm wrong, but doesn't your deity clearly state in the II Peter: 'promising them freedom, while they themselves are slaves of corruption; for by what a man is overcome, by this he is enslaved'? You, sir, are overcome with the obsession of freedom. You are overcome by it and are thus enslaved to freedom."

Jim: "That's outrageous! You're twisting God's words to try and bring me down!"

Isaac: "Am I? Look at it for a minute, without emotion. You and your followers are constantly thinking of freedom. You fight for freedom, but to what end? *Every day* you have to fight to survive, to fight for the Almighty Dollar so that you can have something that others don't. If you gain, someone else has to lose. There is a definitive supply of money. Your gain directly results in someone else's loss. If everyone went to college, if everyone" using his fingers in the quotation marks motion "'bettered themselves' as you like to say, it wouldn't work. There is a finite supply of money and resources. Your alleged freedom distributes these resources in unequal portions, leaving many out, leaving everyone fighting for and chasing an empty, unsustainable dream that many will not reach."

Jim: "Freedom is a basic human right. We are not slaves to freedom. We want to be able to choose our paths. Yes, I understand that there is a finite number of resources and that not everyone can have everything, but those who want to work for something are rewarded, so if Joe works harder than Mary, he is rewarded with more things, and vice versa. It's better to have less and be free to choose what you have and what you do."

Isaac: "And what about the homeless, the starving, the people without work? Your system has no way to avoid these great tragedies, and don't tell me they want to be homeless or they want to be poor, or that they're all drug addicts with no initiative! That is an outdated viewpoint. There are a lot of hard working souls out there that your system has failed. My system will bring equality to all. There will be no homeless, no one going to bed hungry, no one being a slave to trying to keep their status. It will be a true Utopia."

Jim: "That's unrealistic! People are independent. Under your system, they will be slaves to the Government, unable to do anything without your say-so. They will be miserable! People do not like to be told what to do. Look at the case, right here in America, in New Harmony, Indiana. In 1814, they decided to build a utopian society, much like you suggest. It was a total failure! Everyone was miserable. The economy totally collapsed, and they disbanded only a few years later."

Isaac: "Really? Is that the best you can come up with? That was over two hundred years ago, and yet that one town was a pioneer. It produced the first public library *and* the first public school! It made this entire nation better, and now, we will take this one town's experience across the whole country. Justice will be to all, and furthermore, people are not slaves to the government. We are taking away slavery, slavery to simply trying to live and have food, water, and shelter. These are no longer going to be concerns. People will be freer now than they ever have been. We will enter a new Golden Age, where everyone has the necessities of life and survival will no longer be an everyday struggle. These will not have to be thought of."

Jim: "So, you will give everyone a test so you can assign them a job that they very likely will hate. You will tell them what to wear, what to eat, and where to live, how many, if any, children they can have, what doctor, what dentist, everything! You will control every aspect of their lives, and there will be no escape."

Isaac: "They will be happier not having to worry about these things and not having to try and be 'better than the Jones.'"

Jim: "Without freewill, people will be just like animals in cages. There is no sustained happiness in that. We were made by God as free beings." Isaac shakes his head as Jim continues, "We will not be happy unless we are free. That, my friend, is a fact! I may not be able to prove it, but it is the truth. If you win, you will find this out."

Isaac: "Well Jim, I didn't expect a full conversion over dinner, but, you will see. In time, you will be enlightened that mine is the better way, free from envy, strife, chaos, and the constant struggle to remain or move up in class, and, for millions, even finding food or housing."

Jim: "Utopian socialism is not the right way. Freedom is the only path to prosperity and happiness."

Isaac: "Jim, I've got one more history lesson for you about World War II, your favorite era, American capitalism's crowning achievement, as you say."

Jim: "Yes, it was our proudest moment. We, as freedom fighters, saved the world yet again, capitalism at work."

Isaac: "Does the 1942 War Production Act, signed by the great Franklin D. Roosevelt, mean anything to you?"

Jim: "It was a necessary war-time decree to temporarily help us unify the war effort."

Isaac: "Ok, Jim, think about it. The government took control of *all* manufacturing and rationed out most resources with coupons. America was in a crisis, and the outcome of the war would affect the entire future of the planet. It was a war that should have been diplomatically solved, but we went a different path. So, under this path, we had to be victorious. Capitalism simply didn't work. We *had* to move to socialism to survive. It is, in fact, the better way. Your capitalistic crowning achievement was, in effect, solved by socialism."

Jim moves back, visibly disturbed, and takes a deep breath. "I see, Isaac, that you fully believe in your cause and have researched history quite well to help you make your conclusions, but remember, people need to be free. After the war, we ended the War Production Act and capitalism thrived. If you cage people in long enough, they will revolt. We are born to be free, and that, sir, is something that for some reason you cannot understand, and in the long run, it will prove to be your downfall."

Isaac briefly looks at a clock on the wall and tells Jim in such a way as to wrap up the conversation, "I can see you're in an emotionally defensive state right now. We will have plenty of time to talk in the coming months as we work together to better America. I appreciate and respect your views and look forward to working with you. I need to go work on my speech. I'll see you later on tonight. Thanks for the wonderful conversation during dinner!" Isaac gets up, shakes Jim's hand, and walks out. As Jim is left sitting there, he shakes his head and finishes his meal.

After a few minutes Jim gets up, goes to an elevator, and presses the button for the tenth floor. When it reaches his floor he gets off the elevator and walks down the hall to his room. When he gets there, he sees two guards standing in front of his door. He asks them, "Gentlemen, is this really necessary?"

A guard answers him saying, "Sorry sir. We have direct orders from Pablo Martinez to make sure you stay in your room all night."

Jim: "And this is the way you Utopians want to live, without freedom?"

The other guard chimes in, "Ours is the better way, sir."

Jim sighs, walks into his room, and turns on the TV to the Republican Network, which shows a reporter at a news desk, with charts, political maps, and a countdown clock. Jim increases the TV volume to a very loud setting, so the guards can't hear what he is doing. He then pulls out a set of blueprints from his jacket pocket and puts it on his bed and starts studying them. After about an hour, he folds the blueprints back up and puts them into his pocket. After that he goes into the bathroom and finds an air duct above the counter. He climbs up onto the counter, pulls out a screw driver from his suit jacket pocket, and starts to unscrew the vent door. When the vent door is open, he climbs up into the air duct and starts crawling. He crawls a very long distance, making several turns. Eventually he sees an open vent door. He climbs through it, and lands quietly onto a bathroom counter, where he finds a man standing there, waiting on his arrival.

The man smiles at Jim and says, "I see you found your way through the maze of air ducts!"

Jim: "Johnny, those blueprints you gave me were perfect. Do you have the disguise?"

"Of course, sir; it, along with everything else you need to become Daniel Murphy, is on the bed," Johnny says.

Jim then climbs down off the counter, walks over to the bed, grabs the stuff, and goes back into the bathroom to put on a realistic wig and beard, glasses, a jogging suit, and a headband. He also puts on antiperspirant. He walks out of the bathroom and asks, "What do you think?"

Johnny: "Perfect, I don't see how anyone could recognize you."

Jim looks at himself in a full length mirror in the bedroom and says, "This just might work – my compliments to TNN! You have the ID?"

Johnny hands it to him, along with a wallet containing a driver's license, credit cards, Social Security card, and pictures of Murphy's wife and kids, plus a family photo with Jim spliced in. "You are now Daniel Murphy, reporter from the Mobile Press-Register newspaper in Alabama."

Jim looks in the wallet, "Great, Johnny. I think this covers it, wish me good luck!"

Johnny: "Good luck, but here's hoping you won't need it!" Jim starts to walk out, but Johnny catches him, saying, "Oh, wait, let me have your phone. Take this one instead. It belongs to Daniel Murphy. Maghee is standing by, waiting on your call to knock out the hotel surveillance satellite. The second you give the ok, they're blind."

Jim: "Great, has the scrambler been installed?"

Johnny: "Yes sir. Everything's ready to go."

Jim nods to him and walks out the door and into the hallway. He enters the elevator from the ninth floor and pushes the button for the ground level. The elevator starts going down, passing Level 8 but stops on Level 7. The door opens, and Pablo, Isaac, and two body guards enter the elevator. Jim is startled by this, and feels almost queasy.

Isaac reaches out his hand to Jim, saying, "Good day, my friend."

Jim, using his best Alabama accent, which isn't bad, replies, "Mr. President, what a great honor to meet you! I'm Dan Murphy."

Isaac: "The pleasure is mine." Feeling something is off, Isaac looks Jim up and down and asks, "Have I met you before?"

Jim: "I'm a reporter for the Mobile Press-Register. I've covered a few of your speeches, but I have never had the opportunity to ask any questions."

Pablo: "Hmm that must be it. You look familiar to me too. Pablo Martinez." He reaches out and shakes Jim's hand.

Jim: "Pleased to meet you too, sir!" The elevator starts going down.

Isaac puts his hand against the back elevator wall and leans against it. He looks at Pablo as he asks, "Well, Pablo, with the results looking to be closer than we anticipated, are you going to be able to handle everything?"

Pablo: "Oh, yes sir, I've got it all under control."

Isaac: "I'm sure you do. It's just that I've got an uneasy feeling about tonight. Something just doesn't feel quite right."

Pablo: "No problems, sir. All is under control; I put guards outside Jim Taylor's room, to make doubly sure he gives his concession speech." A nervous Jim takes a breath.

Isaac: "Guards?! Why do you have guards?"

The elevator door opens. Jim motions with his arm, "After you, Mr. President."

Isaac: "No, no, after you." He looks over at Jim, and asks, "Are you ok? You look a little flushed."

Jim: "I just need a little fresh air, and to be honest, I'm a little nervous standing in your midst. Thank you, sir, I'm ok." They exit the elevator, and Jim walks down the hall. Isaac and Pablo go in a different direction from Jim.

Jim then walks to the hotel's main door, where, once again, there are two guards. When he approaches the revolving door, a guard stops him and says, "We're limiting traffic into and out of the hotel tonight, sir. Is there a valid reason why you are leaving the hotel?"

Jim: "Yes, there is! I plan on taking an hour-long jog."

The second guard says, "I don't think you need to that. There are exercise facilities in this hotel."

Jim: "I can't handle treadmills. I need the open air."

The second guard replies, "No jogging tonight, sir. You can miss one night. With President Wolfe here, we need to monitor guest access. I'm sure you can understand that."

Jim: "I certainly can, but you don't understand my *problem*, see – are you *married*, by any chance?"

"Well, yes, but what does that have to do with it?"

Jim pulls out his wallet and shows the guards the pictures, points to the wife. "You see her? My darling's *obsessed* over a healthy lifestyle. See, I've picked up ten pounds this year, being on the road so much, so she has put me on a strict 1800-calorie diet and exercise regimen, which includes me jogging for an hour a day, EVERY day!"

"I don't see her here. Just *tell* her you went jogging."

Jim shakes his head and continues, "It don't work that way. You see, I have to call her the moment I start jogging and keep her on the phone the whole hour. She needs to hear me jogging and panting. Believe me, if there was ANY way out of this, I would have found it!"

The first guard: "Are you serious?"

The second guard looks at the first and says, "You're not married. You can't understand! I say we let him go."

The first guard: "I'm not so sure. Maybe we should call Martinez and see what he thinks."

Jim: "I'll only be gone one hour, and I'll stay close to the hotel."

The second guard answers, "That'll work. We have surveillance cameras encompassing two miles of this area. But, be warned, we will keep an eye on you, sir. If you do anything suspicious, you will be apprehended."

The first guard: "I need to me see your ID, so I can log this." Jim hands him his fake driver's license.

"Daniel Murphy, from Alabama, huh? Let me run this through my computer." He pulls out a handheld and scans the driver's license. "So, what is it you say you do, Mr. Murphy?"

Jim: "I'm a reporter for the Press-Register, been there for fifteen years."

"Hmm, that checks out ok, but be back in *one hour*."

Jim: "Thank you! I really appreciate this, sir. You have no idea how much this means to me!" Jim walks out the revolving door, and starts jogging. He pulls out his phone and dials. When he gets Maghee he says, "Hello, Patricia, my love! I've started my jog, and I'm right on schedule, 8 pm, just like I said I would."

Maghee: "Patricia? Are you being followed?"

Jim: "I'm pretty sure I am, dear. I'm about two minutes from the park."

Maghee: "Perfect. Let me know the second you enter the park, and I'll knock out the satellite."

Jim: "Great, dear, that sounds good. I miss you too."

The two guards are watching him. The first guard says to the second, "This is too unbelievable for him to be making it up! Can you imagine talking to your wife while you're jogging? How could anyone live without freedom like that?"

The second guard responds, "Marriage is complicated, but that's really bad! I couldn't live like that either, I feel sorry for him."

Jim: "Well, honey, I'm rounding the corner."

Maghee: "Are you there yet?"

Jim: "I see the park. There are birds everywhere. It's not too bad out here tonight."

Maghee: "I'm shooting down the satellite now. In exactly twenty seconds, make a break into the park. They'll be blind by then."

Jim smiles as he says, "Sure thing honey, I can hardly wait to get back home to you, too."

Over the skies of Texas, a stealth jet fighter is flying above the clouds. Maghee, on the radio, shouts "Now!"

The pilot quickly responds "Yes sir, General." Then he pushes a button, causing the plane to make a loud noise. Fire goes shooting out the back of the jet, causing the plane to zip into outer space. It approaches a satellite, the pilot pushes another button, a red dot lights up and starts blinking on the middle of the satellite. It starts blinking faster, then a huge red light hits it, and then it explodes. The satellite catches fire and starts spiraling down to earth, with parts falling out on the way down. It plunges into the ocean on fire, nearly hitting a Korean fishing boat, and causing it to rock.

Back in D.C. in the hotel, the surveillance screen that the guards were watching goes blank. The second guard asks the first, "What just happened?"

The first replies, "Looks like we've lost power to the surveillance cameras. Get George on the phone – we need to get this fixed now!"

Jim makes a mad dash through the park. He runs to the end of the park and goes into the street, where a car pulls up. He opens the door and jumps in the back seat, and the car speeds away. The driver briefly looks back to Jim and tells him, "Glad you made it, Jim!"

Jim: "Thanks, Tim. A couple of times I thought I was going to get caught."

Tim: "The airport is a little less than an hour and a half from here. I'm still not confident there won't be any roadblocks, besides the tollbooths, between here and there, but the private plane is fueled and ready to go to Austin."

Jim looks at the car clock, "It's 8:30 Eastern, now, and if the plane takes off by 10:30, we'll be in Austin by 1 am Central. That will be cutting it closer than I like, but we should still make it. What's the latest on the numbers?"

Tim: "That's also very close, sir. I think you're going to win the popular vote."

Jim: "How's the electoral looking? Twenty-six polls should have closed by now. How's Ohio?"

Tim: "Ohio is still too close to call. We might have a chance to win! You're up in the states that close early, and networks have you winning 120-83, with 67 up for grabs."

Jim: "I'd really like to give a victory speech instead of a Declaration of Independence speech, but we need to be honest with ourselves. We *have* to keep a good lead because at 11 pm, Isaac automatically gets 70 votes from the West Coast."

8:45

At 8:45 that evening Isaac enters his war room, followed by his entourage. He walks over to Pablo and the rest of his cabinet members, who are standing in the center of a conference room, watching several TVs, each showing election results from a different network. He turns to Eric and asks, "With Arkansas closed, Eric, what are the latest numbers?"

Eric: "They just declared Arkansas Jim's. With polling closed in twenty states, we're down 126-83, and Florida, Ohio, and Pennsylvania are still too close to call."

Isaac gives a surprised look as he asks, "What do you mean, 'too close to call'? We were ahead by ten points in our polling in each of those states! What is going on?"

Eric: "I don't know, sir. In every state, we are receiving fewer votes than our polls had projected."

Isaac suddenly feels faint. His face turns pale, and, all his strength leaves him, forcing him to lean on a desk. He shudders as he says, "Jim must have been right. People *were* afraid to say they were voting for him."

Pablo: "What do you mean? What did Taylor say?"

Isaac: "At dinner Jim said we were perceived as an oppressive government and that people would be afraid to admit to voting against us. He said he had at least a 5% deviation."

Eric: "It looks like he may've been right. Every state, every single state, has had a 5-15% push towards Jim."

Isaac sits down before saying, "So, it's possible we could actually lose this election, then?"

Eric: "Oh, yes sir! The numbers are looking a little dismal right now, although we *were* supposed to win by a landslide. This is setting up to be one of the closest elections in US history."

Isaac stares at him as he says, "Is there any particular reason you sound so happy about this, Eric?"

Sheepishly, Eric replies, "Uh... no, sir."

Pablo: "This is going to make *my* job even more difficult. With this close of an election, there are going to be riots, even if Jim is elected." He then puts his head down and rubs the back of his neck as he says, "I need to go make a few calls," while walking over to his station.

Isaac: "Ok, do what you can, Pablo. Maintaining civil peace is of upmost importance. I know that this election is an emotional one for many, as it is going to change the landscape of America forever. I believe we are going to win this election, and we are going to make this a better world!"

A few minutes later Eric says, "The 9 pm polls are closing soon, so by 9:30, we should have a better idea of how this night is going to go. We know we're going to lose Texas, but if we get Colorado and Wisconsin, we should be in good shape." He then walks out of the room.

Isaac: "Yes, and the polls had us up in those states too, by 10%. So, even with a 5% bounce for Jim, we should still be ok."

9:30

At 9:30 Eric walks back into the room, and Isaac immediately asks him, "It's 9:30, what have you got for me?"

Eric looks down for a moment, then says, "It's not good, sir. Colorado is going to go to Jim, and Wisconsin is going to be just like Florida, Ohio, and Pennsylvania, which are still too close to call. They could all very easily go to Jim. Right now, we're standing at 209 for Jim, to 143 for us. Jim only needs 63 more electoral votes. If he wins Florida, Pennsylvania, and Ohio, we've lost, but there are still eleven states out west whose polls have not closed yet."

Matthew: "Well, the good news is that we should get an automatic 70 votes from California, Washington, and Hawaii. I see no way we lose those states."

Eric: "Yep, we're up by 30-40% in every one of those states. Those are guaranteed."

Isaac: "Nothing is guaranteed tonight, Eric. Something is terribly wrong. I can't put my finger on it, but I've had this bad feeling all day."

Samantha: "Let's add in the automatic states out west. What's it look like with those?"

Eric: "Well, if we add in the 70 electoral votes from those three states, we're ahead right now, 213 to 209."

10:00

On Jim's private plane, he is on the phone with Jacob, saying, "Okay, Jacob, it's about 10 pm. The polls in Iowa, Montana, Nevada, and Utah oughta be closing. Give me good news about Iowa, I want that state!"

Jacob: "I wish I could, Jim, but it's too close to call. So is Nevada, but Utah and Montana are in our corner."

98

Jim: "What's the count now?"

Jacob: "218 to 143, with 89 up for grabs."

Jim: "We just might pull this out yet! The American people are responding. Never give up hope on their need for freedom!"

Jacob: "Remember, though, the West Coast is automatically Isaac's."

In a frustrated tone Jim replies, "Yes, I know! California, with its 55 electoral votes, evens this up right now. That's why states like Iowa are so important. If we can win some of the toss-up states, it's our election, and I'm giving a victory speech and not a Declaration of Independence speech. How is it looking in the earlier three toss-up states? We should have more information by now."

Jacob: "There is no progress on Florida or Ohio. It'll be well into the morning before those are declared. You know that. Unfortunately, Pennsylvania will probably be called to Isaac any moment now, so we lose those important 20 votes, leaving only Wisconsin, Iowa, and Nevada, all too close to call."

Jim: "I was just campaigning in Iowa and Nevada. I have a real good feeling we're going to win those. The yearning for freedom was in the air, I could sense it. They're true Americans in those states!"

Jacob: "I hope you're right, Jim. We really need those states! At 11 the western polls close, and we're going to lose most of those."

Jim: "Idaho and North Dakota are solid, and I'm praying for Oregon. We have a slight chance there."

11:00

Back in Isaac's war room, Eric shouts, "Finally, 11 pm, the best hour of the day! California should be called any minute. Our exit polls there are phenomenal, the same with Washington and Hawaii."

Isaac: "How is Oregon looking?"

Eric: "Well, the exit polls show us ahead by 5%, so the way this night is going, that makes this even."

A nervously pacing Isaac says, "We need Oregon. We need EVERY vote. This is way too close! I never dreamed it would be this close."

Pablo: "This is a nightmare. This is the worst way tonight could have gone. The riots are going to be awful!"

Isaac walks over to Pablo and puts his hand on his shoulders as he says, "Now let's not panic, Pablo. You have the situation under control, don't you?"

Pablo looks in Isaac's eyes and whines, "Sir, I've done the best I could. We have taken every single preventive step we possibly could, and the National Guard is on standby, ready to act. There is nothing else I can do at this point, except hope that you win big at the end *and* win the popular vote."

Eric turns to Pablo as he says, "*That's* not looking good, by the way."

Pablo stares at Eric, "We *have* to win the popular vote. Otherwise, it will incite Jim's people. If they lose the election and win the popular votes, riots will be increased two-fold! How bad does it look?"

Eric: "Even with the big push from Cali, it's looking bleak. For some reason, they didn't come out and vote in the numbers we were hoping for."

Isaac walks over to Eric and asks in an even more annoyed tone, "Just how bleak are we talking, Eric?"

Eric: "Well Isaac, it looks like we will definitely lose the popular vote. At best, it's going to be a 70 million to 70 million tie, but I think it's going to go 71 to 69 in favor of Jim."

A disgusted Isaac shoots Eric a look for the way he's acting so happy to see Jim doing well, before asking him, "So, more people are voting for Jim than for the Utopian way?"

A visibly upset Pablo says, "I've got to go make a few more calls." Before letting out a heavy sigh and storming out of the room.

Isaac sits down on a couch and stares at the ground with a sick look on his face, saying in a weak voice, "How could I have misinterpreted the wishes of the American people that badly? What did I do wrong?"

Samantha sits down next to him, and puts her arm around him, "I don't think it's you. I think Jim Taylor has gotten everyone emotional, and people are voting irrationally, based on emotion. Don't worry, Isaac, they'll come around."

Visibly relieved, Isaac looks at Samantha as he says, "Yes, you're right. Thanks, Samantha, for being the voice of reason. We are going to win this election by the electoral votes, and those are the only votes that count. The people will eventually calm down and recognize that ours is the better way."

Eric: "Not to interrupt this sweet moment you two are having, but it was just declared that California, Washington, and Hawaii are ours, and Jim got Idaho and North Dakota."

Isaac stands up asking, "What's the count?"

Eric: "We've closed the gap to 225 to 214, and Pennsylvania should be declared ours any minute now. That will give us the lead, 234 to 228.

Samantha shouts with exuberance, "We got it – they just called it!"

Isaac shouts with excitement and joy, "Finally, the first lead we've had all night!" With hope in his voice he continues, "Give me more good news! What about Florida, Ohio, Wisconsin, and Iowa?"

Eric: "Well, Florida and Ohio are in chaos, sir. They don't think they'll know the result until at least 4 am, but Wisconsin should go our way soon."

Isaac: "I noticed you avoided Iowa."

Eric takes a deep breath before he speaks because he knows Isaac won't like what he will say. "Looks like it's going Jim's way, but it's still a close race, with 95% of the precincts having reported in."

12:30

In Jim's plane, still en route to Texas, Jim calls Jacob one last time before he lands, "Well Jacob, it's 12:30 Eastern. I'm about to land in a few minutes and should be in Austin in forty minutes or so. What's it looking like right now?"

Jacob: "We still have no idea about Florida and Ohio, but the other states have all been called, except of course, for Alaska, whose polls don't close for another half-hour."

Jim: "Well, Alaska is solid Republican. Did Iowa and Nevada go our way?"

Jacob: "Yes, they did, but Wisconsin and Oregon were called for Isaac."

Jim: "Ok, let's add Alaska to our total. What are the numbers, not counting Florida and Ohio?"

Jacob: "We're down 251 to 240, but if we win *both*, we win the election."

Jim: "It's even easier than that. It all comes down to Florida."

Jacob: "How's that? We need 270 or an act of Congress to win. Florida only gives us 269."

Jim: "Yes, and if Ohio goes to Isaac, it's a 269 to 269 tie, but we *don't* go to socialism."

Jacob: "How's that? It would be a tie."

Jim: "The 12th Amendment, Jacob! Remember the Constitution, that quaint little document we've been trying so hard to protect? It goes to Congress, and the House will vote for President. Each state gets one vote, so whoever gets the majority of House votes from that state would get its vote. At least two out of three of the states *have* to vote. If they can't decide and it remains a tie, the Vice President automatically becomes President."

Jacob: "Yes, Jim, you're right. I knew that! What we need to know, in that case, is how the Congressional election has gone tonight. I've been focused solely on the Presidential election."

Jim: "I was able to check that while I was in Washington. We have 28 states, with a Republican majority in the House. We win at least 28 to 22, so if it comes down to the Congressional vote, I will be the new President."

Jacob: "Yeah, but, I won't be the new Vice President."

Jim: "I'm afraid not, Jacob. The 12th Amendment states that the VP is selected by the Senate. Since it takes 51 out of the 100 votes, and the Senate is still going to be probably 52 to 48 in favor of the Democrats and Socialists, Isaac will probably be my VP – that is, IF we don't win Ohio also."

Jacob: "Let's hope we win them both, but at the very least, Florida!"

Jim: "Yes, let's hope so! What are the latest numbers on Florida?"

Jacob: "You have the lead now, but several precincts in Miami have not fully reported in yet."

Jim: "Let's hope they had a small turnout, as we know that most of them are going to vote for the Socialists. I've got a nagging feeling in my gut that the question isn't 'Do you think we can hang on?' but rather 'Will Isaac's supporters keep it clean?!'"

Jacob: "It's going to be close, as close as the 2000 election, when Bush barely beat Gore. Now, THAT was controversial!"

Jim: "I don't want controversy, but we need to win. Ok, I'm getting ready to land, catch up with you in about thirty minutes."

1:30

Back in Isaac's war room, Isaac asks Eric, "Ok, Eric, it's 1:30 am. What are the latest numbers?"

Eric: "Well, Ohio is really close, but 99% of the precincts are in. We should know in a few minutes about that state. Florida still has 3% of the votes not reporting, and every other state has been called. Right now we are ahead, 251 to 240."

Isaac: "We *need* to get Florida."

Samantha: "Ohio will guarantee us a tie."

Eric: "They just called Ohio – worst case scenario, it's a tie!"

Samantha cheers, "All right!" People all around the room start clapping and giving high-fives, but Isaac is looking down. Samantha looks at Isaac and asks, "What's wrong, Isaac? You're not celebrating. We took Ohio, so you've at least got a tie."

Isaac: "I'm very glad to have Ohio, but you guys have to remember the rules. If we lose Florida, Socialism has lost. America has lost, and I'll go so far as to say that the world has lost. Under this outdated Constitution that we currently use, the 12th Amendment will give Jim the election."

Eric: "How?! It would be a tie. He wouldn't win."

Isaac gives Eric a very disappointed look before saying, "You didn't just ask me that, Eric!" Isaac looks around the room, seeing confused looks on everyone's faces. He shouts, "Can *anybody* tell me what the 12th Amendment says?" After several seconds of complete silence, Isaac takes a deep breath before explaining to the entire room, "Look, the Constitution is outdated, there's no denying it. But, it's been the law of the land since the US was in its infancy. The 12th Amendment states that if it's a tie, the Presidency is decided by the House of Representatives. Each state gets one vote, and at least 2/3 of the states *have* to vote for the President. If the House can't reach a decision by March 4th, next year, the Vice President automatically becomes President."

Eric: "Uh-oh, there are twenty-eight states controlled by Republicans and Conservatives. There's no way we can win. We need Florida!"

Isaac: "You see my point?" He pauses for a second and then asks, "What's Florida looking like?"

Eric: "This is as close as the 2000 election. I have no idea how this is going to go! Jim is leading now, but our friends from Miami haven't all been counted, but we know they will vote in heavy numbers for us. Right now, it's just a matter of how many of them came out and voted."

Isaac: "Well, it was sunny all day in Miami, so hopefully, they came out."

Samantha: "What are you going to do if we lose?"

Isaac: "I don't know. It would be a terrible loss for the entire world! It could be generations before someone else is able to bring socialism to America. It would be a terrible tragedy, so let's hope our friends in Miami win the day for us!"

2:00

At the Texas Governor's Mansion in Austin, Jim is looking at papers, and pacing as he talks to Jacob, who is sitting at a table. Jim says, "It's 2 am, Eastern. Has Florida been called yet?"

Jacob: "It's still too close to call, Jim. There's been no progress. Nobody has any idea. We're still ahead, but each set of votes coming in is going to Isaac."

Jim laughs, shaking his head "no," "I can't believe this. Miami is deciding the future of America! It's just not right."

Jacob: "Well, everyone has had the opportunity to vote."

Jim: "I know, but Miami isn't like the rest of America. The situation there is completely different. It's a different culture, a socialistic one. I just hope that for some reason, they didn't come out in good numbers. Was there anything to hinder them from going out and voting?"

In a whiny tone of voice Jacob replies, "No, the weather was great and the Socialists were giving out free food and busing people into the polls all day long."

Jim throws his papers on table shouting, "That's just not right! It's bribery, plain and simple: 'vote for me and get a free meal.' I bet most of them don't even know who George Washington was, nor can they site one line out of the Constitution."

Jacob carrying on with his whiny tone, "I know Jim... I know, but we have a minor chance to win." He starts speaking more confidently as he continues, "If you do become President, you can inspire everyone to love the Constitution, love our country, and keep America alive!"

Jim: "You're right, Jacob. We can do that. When we're in charge, we'll promote capitalism instead of socialism and gradually change the views of people so that they will start to love our country like we do."

Jacob: "Now, that's the Jim Taylor I know!"

Jim: "This is painfully slow, with still only 98% of the votes in, but Isaac is closing in fast. I wish we could just finish counting these votes and end this torture."

3:00

Back in Isaac's war room, Isaac is pacing and looks to Eric as he says, "There has to be 100% of the votes in by now. Tell me we have Florida!"

Eric: "They're calling it as we speak!"

On TV a jubilant reporter is announcing, "And now, for the announcement we've all been waiting for, we are ready to call Florida. After all the votes are in, the winner is Socialism, and our new Czar, Isaac Wolfe!" Everybody in the room is ecstatic, with cheers, applause, whistling, and papers being tossed into the air, people hugging each other, giving of high-fives, and merriment all around.

Isaac walks towards the door, "This was much closer than what it should have been. We are going to have a lot of work to do." He points to Pablo, and continues, "Pablo, stay on top of everything and keep me informed. I'm going to go give my speech." Then he points with his other hand, "Eric, go find Jim and have him ready to give his concession speech. *Great* job everyone, we pulled it off!" Isaac then walks out of the room and down the hall.

A few seconds after Florida is called, General Maghee ends a conference call by shouting, "Ok, now, everyone make it quick and clean. Follow the plan; we don't have much time! You hear me? Quick and clean!" Several people respond, "Sir, yes sir!" Then, Maghee hangs up the phone.

Immediately, a Special Ops unit in New York secures the Statue of Liberty to steel ropes attached to a helicopter hovering above. They finish tying the ropes, jump off the base, run to the water, and swim to a nearby submarine, which surfaces and shoots a laser, separating the statue from its base, and the helicopter lifts the statue. The pilot says, "Ya know, I can't believe we actually have to do this." The submarine opens a large door to receive the statue. A couple of people gently guide the statue into place inside the submarine. Then, the helicopter lands inside the submarine also. The door closes, and the submarine dives back into the water and then takes off at great speed.

While this is happening, at the National Archives Building, three agents Patrick, Barbara, and Randy, disguised as security officers are walking down a hallway. Barbara says to her team "Ok, Maghee said 'quick and clean.' Lucky for us, all of the documents have been placed together by Wolfe's people in anticipation of the change in government!"

They walk at a fast pace into a room. Randy pushes buttons to disable cameras and alarms and then stands guard. After Randy disables them, Patrick cuts into a glass case, making a big circle. Patrick and Barbara pull the cut glass out gently. Then, Barbara hands off the glass to Patrick and reaches in and pulls out the documents, putting them in a protective cylinder that she was carrying. She then replaces the documents with fakes. Patrick puts the glass circle back and repairs it with a spray. Barbara then says to her team, "Ok, that's the Declaration of Independence, the Constitution, the Bill of Rights, and the Magna Carta. Let's get back up to the south side, quick, and make contact." Randy turns the alarms and footage back on, and they walk quickly out a door. They meet two people standing there, Chad and Michelle.

Chad says, "Washington."

Patrick replies, "Lincoln."

Michelle says, "Reagan."

Randy replies, "Jefferson."

Barbara: "Perfect. Those are the four correct words in order." She gives the protected cylinder cases to Chad, who runs away immediately.

Meanwhile, at the Liberty Bell Center, a plain truck pulls up, and a special agent opens the French doors in the back of the truck. Immediately, a plain dark blue van pulls up, and ten special operatives get out of the van. They climb up the building and start unhinging the bell. A cushioned ramp extends from the back of the truck upward thirty feet ending next to the bell. Four of the operatives get on the ramp. The driver asks on radio, "Ok, ready?"

The leader replies, "Affirmative, sending it to you now." The agents guide the bell down the ramp and into the truck. Once the bell is inside, the cushioned ramp is mechanically drawn back into the cushioned bed of the truck. The group gets back into their vehicles, and the truck takes off, with the van following behind. The people in the van are carrying machine guns and grenade launchers, looking out the windows guarding.

Back in Austin, Jim and Jacob are in a room watching TV, about to watch Isaac's victory speech. Jim shakes his head before saying, "It's unbelievable that we lost this election. Socialism has been shoved down American's throats."

Jacob: "Well, we did win the popular vote, by 2 million."

Jim: "Which means, the majority of Americans want to keep capitalism. It will make our chances for success greater, so, in that way, it's actually good news. We won't be able to change the mindset of people in California, much of New York, and the rest of the Northeast for generations. Maybe it's better if they go their own way. Everyone who wants to be a *true* American will have that chance, and those that don't can stay with Isaac and be oppressed. In about twenty minutes, America will be revived and will live on for centuries."

Jacob: "It's not going to be easy. Isaac is not going to take this very well. He's about to speak now."

On TV Isaac is standing at a podium speaking: "My fellow Utopians, we are entering into a new age, a true Utopia, where everyone will have everything they need. No longer will the little children go to bed hungry. No longer will millions of you have to be homeless, wondering how you are going to make it to tomorrow. No more will you be oppressed by the corporate slave drivers making you work fourteen-hour days in order to try to survive. No more will you have to worry about finding employment. No longer will you have to go without the basic necessities of life, while the rich live in lavish luxury, not caring about your plight. We will all be equal! We will all have what we need, and we will all be happy! We now have a Utopian Society. Thank you for your votes, thank you for your support for bettering the world. Today, you have made the difference. You have created Utopia!" A crowd is shown in front of his podium cheering wildly. Balloons and confetti are falling, with joyful music playing.

Jim sighs as he turns off the TV and turns to Jacob, saying, "Well, Isaac is pretty happy right now, but it's time to put a stop to that. He's probably got people looking for me in my hotel room right now. It's time to give the speech to save America. The TV cameras are all set up in the next room. Let's go, Jacob." They get up and walk down a hallway.

Meanwhile in Utopia, Isaac is curious as to Jim's whereabouts. He walks away from his podium and goes behind a curtain to call Eric. He asks, "Hey, Eric, where is Jim?"

Eric replies, "I don't know. He's not answering his door."

Isaac sighs before answering, "Ok, I'll be right up." Accompanied by secret service, he walks over to an elevator, goes up to Jim's floor, walks to Jim's room, where he meets Eric and two guards outside. He knocks on the door and says, "I know you're in there, Jim, open up! We have an agreement."

Eric stands next to Isaac and says, "I told you, he's not answering."

Isaac turns to the guards and asks them, "He didn't leave tonight, did he?"

One of the guards replies, "No sir, we have been here all night, and we have helicopters watching the windows. There's nowhere he could have gone. He has to be in there."

Isaac sighs before saying, "Maybe he's distraught over losing. He could be in bad physical shape; maybe he had a heart attack." He points to the door with his head saying, "Guards, knock down the door. Eric, call medical." The guards kick in the door, and Isaac goes running in. The TV is blasting on the Republican network. Isaac looks around the room asking, "Where is he?"

Eric puts his phone away, "I see a note here on the table."

Isaac stops searching and asks, "A note?" He walks over to the table and asks, "What's it say?"

Eric stoops over to pick it up, reads it, and unenthusiastically says, "It's from Jim. He says, 'Isaac, FREEDOM will NEVER die!'"

Isaac: "What does that even mean? Where is he?"

One of the secret service agents says to Isaac, "Um, sir, I think the TV is about to answer you." He points to it. Isaac walks over to be directly in front of the TV. The bed is behind him.

Announcer: "And now, Jim Taylor."

Jim steps up to the podium and begins. "My fellow Americans, tonight is a night of change."

Isaac talks over to the TV, "Good. He's ok. A little flamboyant, maybe, but he's keeping his end of the bargain. Looks like he's giving his speech, he probably thought it would be best to do it from the Republican Network. Let's hear what he has to say."

Jim continuing on TV, "A time of major change is upon us! Today, we stared into the face of freedom and had a choice to make. Should we give up on freedom and let all of our ancestors' sacrifices for freedom have been for naught? Do we throw that all away and take on a socialist government and become a controlled nation?"

Isaac and Eric look at each other with confused expressions. Isaac asks, "What is he doing? I don't like the way this is going."

Continuing Jim's speech:

"Would our ancestors, who came here and formed this country, throw away freedom? No, they *fought and formed this country* for freedom, and many of them gave their lives to protect it.

"Did our founding fathers run from freedom when they were in danger? No, they stayed the course and fought their motherlands for the good of generations to come!

"Did we back down in World War I and World War II, or run from freedom then? No, Americans stood up and *fought* for freedom!

"Today, when faced with the option of throwing away freedom to begin living under a completely socialistic government, did Americans run away from their responsibilities and choose the new government? NO, the majority did not! Over half of Americans stood up proudly and said "NO, we will NOT be oppressed, and we will NOT bow down to this communistic regime!"

Jim looks directly at the camera, and points to it, continuing, "Isaac, I will NOT let you destroy this country!

We, as FREE American citizens, have voted to keep and maintain our freedoms which are granted to us by the United States Constitution." Jim slams his fist down on his podium, before firmly declaring, "We will NOT lie down and die!"

A totally shocked Isaac falls down on the bed stunned.

Jim continues:

"My fellow Americans, quoting from the Declaration of Independence: '...when a long train of abuses and usurpations, pursuing invariably the same object, evinces a design to reduce them under absolute despotism, it is their *right*, it is their *duty* to THROW OFF such government, and to provide *new* guards for their future security.' Isaac, you and your abusive, destructive, despotic regime have been *thrown off*! Per the Declaration of Independence, we are setting up *new* guards for our future security. As of this very moment, the following states have agreed to remain free; and, to secede if necessary, from your new nation of Utopian Socialists of America; and to remain the United States of America, as we consider this division to be you seceding from us. We are *not* making the switch to this new Utopian Socialist government. These proud states are: Texas, Alabama, Georgia, Tennessee, South Carolina, Oklahoma, Louisiana, Mississippi, Indiana, and Kentucky. Although there are only ten of us, we remain the United States of America, and I know that over the next few days, many more states which voted against your Utopia will come back home to freedom, to regain their status of statehood in the United States of America.

"I encourage each and every one of you who are *true* Americans to *demand* your freedoms and *demand* your state government to come back to where they belong! If any of you are trapped hopelessly in a Utopian territory, I urge you to escape and get to where you belong, where Freedom lives.

"As I speak, the Statue of Liberty is on her way to the Houston Harbor, the Liberty Bell is en route to Atlanta, and the US Constitution and Bill of Rights, as well as the Declaration of Independence and Magna Carta, are in flight to Austin, Texas, which is now the site of freedom's new capital. Freedom and all it stands for will live on, and these symbols of our freedom will also live on. We will not let them be destroyed by the Utopians.

"We will also retain control of the Great Lakes. They are patrolled and secure, and any intrusion by the Utopians will be met with swift and decisive military action."

Isaac has his hands in his face and is looking down.

Jacob walks up to Jim, shielding his face from the camera, and says something to Jim. With vigor in his heart and fire in his eyes Jim continues:

"At this time, I am proud to announce that New Mexico is now our eleventh state! We have successfully secured it, and I am happy to announce to the citizens of New Mexico that you are FREE, you are FREE!!!!

"In addition, let this be a warning to Russia, China, and every other nation, including you, Isaac! I have revived the MX missile system from Utah, and these missiles have been updated and are now fully functional and ready to be let loose on my command. They are safely travelling underground in the free United States of America, protecting our freedom again as they once did under the great leadership of President Ronald Reagan!

Freedom is alive tonight. Freedom is alive, and we will *not* let it die. We ARE the land of the free and the home of the brave, the United States of America!!!!!

"Don't give up hope my friends in the Utopian country. I will be in constant communication with each of your old state leaders, urging them to come back to the freedom of the United States. I will not forget you nor abandon you. I will *not* rest until every one of you who wants to be free is back where you belong, in the greatest country in the history of the world, the United States of America. I urge you again to join us. Come back to where you belong.

"Now, for you good citizens of Florida, I know that 95% of the geographic region has voted to remain free and that only pockets in Tampa and Orlando, along with the great majority of Miami, have voted to go Utopian. I cannot, and will not, allow the whole state to suffer because of basically one city. We have recovered Florida, and it is now part of Georgia, except for the Panhandle, which is now part of Alabama. Yes, my friends in Florida, you are FREE, you are Free!!!! Unfortunately, though, Miami is a lost cause. It will take time that we don't have to convert it to freedom. We have seen so many times over the years that their culture is not one

that prefers freedom, so we will begin shipping
and busing everyone out of Miami to New York,
where they can live the Utopian lives they want.
Everyone must be out by noon on Friday.
That's about fifty-six hours to move five and a
half million people out of the area. We cannot
let Miami continue to be Utopian-minded, as the
Gulf of Mexico is strategic to the United States.
I will not let it fall into Utopian control, just like
the Great Lakes. Any encroachment in the Gulf
by the Utopians, or any other nation, will be met
with swift military retaliation. At noon Friday, I
will authorize the nuclear destruction of Miami.
Anyone who lives within fifty miles of the city
needs to be evacuated. I know this sounds
inhumane and excessive, but we will not tolerate
any threat to freedom. I assure you, this is the
only option we have found.

"We have much work to do. Keep the faith, and
let freedom ring. Good night, my fellow
Americans, and stay strong."

He walks away from the podium and leaves the room.
A horrified Isaac gets up and turns off the TV before saying,
"What is he doing?! This is wrong, completely wrong. He
defends the Constitution, and then doesn't listen to the will of
the American people to switch to a Utopian Society?"

Eric: "He needs to be stopped, sir."

Isaac: "Eric, get everyone together, right now,
downstairs in our meeting room, in fifteen minutes. I want
everyone there!"

In Isaac's war room, Isaac and his cabinet are gathered
around a large conference room table. Isaac starts the meeting

by saying, "Ok, everyone, we have a severe crisis on our hands. Ten states have already seceded, two have been taken over, and I believe eighteen more may leave, one way or the other. Jim has claimed the Great Lakes and the Gulf of Mexico. And, as if that wasn't enough, he says he intends to detonate a nuclear weapon in Miami, and he's not answering my calls."

Pablo: "We need to eliminate him, sir, with a clean assassination, quietly and swiftly."

A visibly annoyed Isaac sighs and replies, "No, Pablo, we can't do that. We need to find a diplomatic solution. Everyone is emotional right now, and nobody's had any sleep tonight, but we need to find a diplomatic solution. I know one must exist."

Eric: "I'm with Pablo. Jim is trouble. He's a traitor to our nation! He's violating the people's will, which was made abundantly clear by the election results."

Samantha: "We can't have Miami evacuated and nuked. We don't have the resources to house five and a half-million people on just two days' notice! They can't just be homeless, because it's too cold outside this time of year. Isaac, you've gotta stop this maniac. I'm with Pablo and Eric, Taylor must be eliminated!"

Isaac: "So, all three of my top advisors can't see diplomacy as an option?"

Pablo: "Look, Isaac, it is *way* past time for diplomacy. Every hour that passes, our country grows weaker. Can you comprehend that Jim now controls the Army, Navy, Marines, and Air and Space Forces? All of the military leaders have joined him, as well as 80% of the troops. And Maghee, don't even get me started on *that* traitor!" He pauses for a moment to take a breath. "Sir, we only have 20% of the military, while he has 80%. If he wants to take us over, there is *no way* we can stop him. We *must* kill him, *now*, sir! There is no other option. I can have a SWAT team do it."

Matthew sighs, "But if we kill him, he'll become a martyr." He slouches in his seat and sighs again before continuing, "We're in a no-win situation."

Isaac: "This is treason, I agree. How can Maghee and the other military leaders just abandon us?"

Matthew: "It looks to me like Jim's been planning this for a long lime, sir."

Pablo: "Look, all of our surveillance satellites are gone. We're blind. Sitting ducks! For all we know, he could be about ready to bomb DC right now. We just don't know!"

Isaac stares at Pablo for a second and replies in a frustrated tone, "Look! He wouldn't destroy DC. That's the seat of what he considers to be *his* country. But, as long as tensions remain so high, he won't think twice about *overthrowing* us in the name of his god Freedom. I just need to talk to him and bring reason back into the picture. I don't think he really wants to do us harm. Diplomacy can still prevail. Right now, emotions are high, and we all need to just calm down." He takes a deep breath, then points his finger aimlessly as he says, "Call a meeting at eight am in the White House Situation room, of all the top government leaders: all of you and our nine remaining District Leaders. We need to meet, *after* we all rest for a couple of hours. We can come up with a plan then. In the next three hours, I will continue trying to get a hold of Jim."

END CHAPTER

CHAPTER FIVE

AMERICA DIVIDED

A little while later, now 5 am Eastern Standard Time, Jim and Jacob are at the Austin Governor's mansion. An exhausted Jacob is sitting on a comfy chair and Jim is standing up, looking at a large touch screen which shows a map of the states. As Jim is looking at the map, Jacob starts a conversation saying, "I think you gave a great speech Jim. I think it went a long way towards uniting America."

Jim: "We need the other states to leave the Utopians right away, while we have the momentum! I'm hoping to be able to get back thirty states by the end of week!" As he finishes talking, Jim's phone starts to ring. Jim pulls it out of his pocket and looks at it.

Jacob asks, "Who is that at five am, Isaac again?"

Jim: "Looks like it's the Arkansas governor." He answers the phone, "Hullo?"

Governor Johnson: "Hey, Jim, this is Joe Johnson."

Jim: "You're calling to say you're joining us?"

Governor Johnson: "You bet, Jim. Our National Guard, alongside many other patriotic Americans, stopped Pablo's group at the border. It's like our state motto says, 'The People Rule.' Please count us in. As far as I'm concerned, the great state of Arkansas never left the Republic."

Jim: "That's great news, Joe!" Jim walks over to Jacob pats him on the shoulder and tells him, "We just got Arkansas!" An exhausted Jacob raises his right fist in triumph with what little enthusiasm he can muster.

Governor Johnson: "Well, if you like that, Jim, I can do ya one even better."

Jim: "I'm listening, Joe, what've ya got for me?"

Governor Johnson: "Missouri and Kansas are onboard too. I've been in constant communication with them both tonight, and they have also stopped Pablo's troops from entering their states." He chuckles before continuing, "It's the first time I've seen Kansas and Missouri work together in years!"

Jim: "That's terrific news! Freedom is even bringing those two together. They've not gotten along since before World War II, if then even. I'm happy to have you three aboard and hoping many of the other states will soon follow. My plan is to start calling up all the states this morning. Talk at ya later, Joe." Jim hangs up and starts dialing Maghee.

Maghee answers, "Maghee here."

Jim: "How's it going?"

Maghee: "Better than expected: Great Lakes and Gulf of Mexico are secure; most, if not all, of Isaac's satellites are destroyed; and, I've had reports that multiple states' National Guard troops have stopped Pablo's invasion at their borders."

Jim: "Wonderful! How many is multiple?"

Maghee: "At least fifteen are resisting."

Jim: "Any conflicts that you had to take care of in the Great Lakes or Gulf?"

Maghee: "Pablo sent a few fighters and some troops. We offered to let them rejoin us, but they declined, so their planes were shot out of the sky, and their troops expired within seconds of entering the United States' borders."

Jim: "Good, any problems?"

Maghee: "Virginia's in bad shape, Jim. It's citizens versus citizens, and Pablo's armies against the state's National Guard. The Utopians don't want to give up this state, but the

Americans who voted for freedom are refusing to submit to the Utopians."

Jim: "Yes, Jacob has been keeping me informed about Virginia. Do you have any suggestions?"

Maghee: "I have two: one, we annex the majority of the state stopping about fifty miles away from DC; or two, we clear a path to Kentucky or Tennessee and move the free people out."

Jim: "How is your troop deployment looking? Do you have enough to safely take over Virginia?"

Maghee: "At this time, we're looking good. We outnumber them 4:1 and have the superior tech. We know where Utopian troops are coming in from. I've been talking with my sources, and I believe that if we fire some tactical missiles, we can wipe out the majority of the Utopian units in the area. Once that's done we could take the state in under an hour. There will be some civilian casualties – that cannot be avoided – but it would be much less than the projected amount if the riots were to continue. Virginia is ours on your word, Jim."

Jim: "Free them, Maghee! By all means, free them now!"

Maghee: "Yes sir!"

Jim hangs up and turns to Jacob, to see him just getting off the phone himself. Jim tells him, "It looks like your state is going to be onboard."

Jacob: "That is *awesome* news! And, on top of that, while you were on the phone, I talked to Santanna Pleasantine. He said North Carolina is once again part of the United States. They were able to easily defeat Pablo's armies."

Jim motions with the triumphant fist and then replies, "Good, this is going better than I had hoped!"

Back in Utopia, 8 am in the White House Situation Room, Isaac, his advisors, and nine of his District Leaders are gathered around a large conference table. Everyone has a name-and-title plate in front of them on the conference table. Alfred Schmidt, from Philadelphia, is wearing a somber look and has a briefcase before him on the table.

Isaac starts the meeting by standing to gain everyone's attention. "Thank you all for coming here in this bleak hour. I know none of us has had any sleep, and we already find ourselves in an emergency situation. As you know, Jim Taylor has led a rebellion in which ten states immediately seceded from our Utopian Society at 3:30 this morning. Since then, four more states have joined them and three others have been captured by them. Based on popular voting results, I believe as many as thirteen more former states either will leave or consider leaving. We have lost all satellite communication, so we are not gathering our normal intelligence, and we basically have no idea what is going on in these states. Personal cell phone calls are the only source of intelligence we have, and I imagine Jim is working on taking down all of our towers as we speak. We are in a grave situation, as our military is outnumbered 4:1, and Jim can completely destroy us if he wishes. Does anyone here have any suggestions?"

Pablo stands and shouts at Isaac, "As I suggested last night, we send in a SWAT team and assassinate Jim this morning, this very morning! Then, when they're in disarray, we can start taking back key states."

Eric nods, "I completely agree."

The Orlando District Leader, Jose Rodriguez, continues the trend by affirming, "Yes, we need to stop this maniac before he nukes Miami!"

Isaac looks down and sighs before replying, "Look, I appreciate your ideas. I really do, but we need to solve this peacefully. Violence will only make things worse."

The District Leader from St. Louis, Terrel Bone, chimes in, "I just got word this morning on the plane ride here that Missouri seceded, so I lost my District Headquarters in St. Louis. Isaac, we have to kill Jim *now* before this gets any further out of hand! By the way, where is Luke? Has Jim taken him out too?" Everyone looks over to the empty seat of Luke Montero of the Salt Lake District.

Isaac looks directly at Terrel Bone, as he answers him, "We don't know where Luke is. As I said, our military intelligence is presently very limited, and we are blind."

District Leader from Detroit, Frank Barker, says "All the more reason to take swift military action *now* – if we don't, we're dead!"

Isaac: "So, all of you are proposing we kill Jim and start a war?"

District Leader from Philadelphia, Alfred Schmidt talking very quickly and sharply, "With all due respect, sir, we're already at war, and time is a luxury we don't have! First thing we need to do is draft 100% of the able bodied citizens to join the military, either working around the clock making weapons or on the front line killing as many of the freedom lovers as they can. We have to set an example. Resistance to our new society ends torturously! Matthew, you need to start converting all buildings to military use. All factories are needed to make tanks, bombers, nuclear weapons, etc. Samantha, you need to start housing workers right by the factories. They need to work eighteen-hour days. I think we can start catching up if everyone fourteen and over, not making weapons, is in the army." He then opens up his briefcase and hands papers to Samantha, Matthew, and Pablo. "I have it planned out right here. If we follow this, within a couple of weeks, this rebellion will be over."

Pablo looks over the papers and exclaims, "This is brilliant!"

Isaac: "Now, wait a minute, guys, let's use our heads here. Everyone is letting emotion guide their judgment. We need to calm down. War is never the answer. Diplomacy is the only route we should ever take."

Alfred Schmidt stands up and pounds his fist on the table as he says, "The time for diplomacy is past, Isaac! If we do not squelch this rebellion, others will rise up against us. We need to defend our people, or we will be conquered."

Isaac says in an almost motherly tone, "Now calm down! Here's what we are going to do. One, I will continue to work on contacting Jim, and when I do get through, I will reason with him. If he loves this country as much as he claims he does, he will listen to reason and not destroy this nation. Two, we will weather the storm. Let the states that secede, secede. We'll get them back diplomatically later on, once emotions have settled down. Three, we will concentrate our efforts on securing the Utopian states that are truly Utopian and move forward with our plans in those old states. And four, for defensive purposes, I have contacted our friends in China, and they are sending troops as we speak to help defend the borders of the true Utopian states that are not seceding. Pablo, I want your complete cooperation with China. Share all military secrets and plans. They have a lot more experience in settling citizen unrest than we do. We can learn from them. We will weather this storm and we will *not* let diplomacy fail!"

Alfred Schmidt is visibly angry, and becomes animated as he speaks, speaking very fast, raising his voice with each word. What?! Have you lost your senses? *You are going to destroy us* by giving China all our military secrets! Ya know, they're secrets for a reason, and the only thing you're going to achieve, by bringing in China, is our total annihilation! And how can you allow Taylor to live and the resistance to grow?" He pauses for a moment and shakes his head. He then motions with his hand at his head that Isaac is insane, shouting, "You're naïve and delusional! Your views are primitive and unrealistic, and you, as a person, are incapable of leading us out of this war that *you* have failed to prevent!"

Isaac motions to his secret service agents, saying, "Security, get him out of here. He is too emotional to be productive."

Security guards grab Schmidt from his chair and carry him out, his feet dragging along the floor as they go. As he's being carried out of the room, he yells, "You have destroyed our government! You *must* be removed from power for America to survive!" They make it through the door, which slams shut behind them.

Isaac takes a deep breath before trying to right the ship by saying, "Sorry about that. I know everyone is emotional right now."

Pablo: "He has some good ideas, sir. I think we *should* attack, and these detailed plans, they're flawless!"

Samantha: "I can make his plans work!"

Matthew: "Isaac, we can start mass producing weapons on your go ahead."

Isaac: "No! Have you people not been listening to anything I've said?! We are going to stay the course and work out a diplomatic solution. We promised the people a Utopian Society, not a war. Let those who want to leave, secede. We will make it work for those who stay. Eventually, everyone will come back, but change is hard. People are more emotional than any of us expected, but together we will get through this!"

District Leader Rodriguez: "What about Miami? It has about two days left before Taylor nukes it."

Isaac: "I doubt he really will, but, in case he does, we need to evacuate everyone. Everything will be ok. We will weather this storm, and diplomacy will win out in the long run."

Eric: "I don't know, Isaac. I don't think we can wait. I'm with Schmidt – we have to act now."

District Leader Bone: "So am I."

District Leader Barker: "Me too."

Isaac: "Is anyone with *me*, here?" Five District Leaders: Tom Rhoades of Los Angeles, Jerrod Michaelson of Boston, Richard Jackson of New York, Tony Sanchez of Seattle, and Henry Pilot of San Francisco, raise their hands.

Henry stands up and says, "We're with you, Isaac. Let's weather this storm and keep our Utopian promises to the people. Let them live and be happy."

District Leader Bone: "That's easy for you guys to say, your borders are secure. I've lost my city, and my entire district is almost gone, maybe even all gone by now."

District Leader Barker: "Hey now, I've got fighter pilots controlling my Great Lakes, Indiana looks like they're building up for an invasion, and as a Michigander I've never trusted Ohio."

Isaac: "Remember, our Chinese friends will help you to secure your borders, Frank. Terrell, I'm going to reassign you to Chicago. I want you and Frank to work closely with the Chinese to keep Jim from invading."

District Leader Bone: "I don't like the sound of working with China. How do we know they won't take us over once they get here and are given all of our military secrets?"

Isaac: "Oh, no, they won't do that. I'm close friends with every member of the Chinese Communist Party. We have had a great working relationship since I first took office. They are my friends and will not harm us."

District Leader Barker: "We can't trust them. They've been planning our destruction for decades!"

Isaac: "Ill-founded rumors, brought on by the capitalistic war mongers. Trust me, they are our allies and have nothing but good intentions for us, as we have for them."

District Leader Bone says loudly, "Yes sir," then whispers under his breath, "But I still don't trust them!"

Isaac: Understand that you have been brainwashed by the Capitalists. Trust will come in time. Does anyone else have any questions, concerns, or suggestions? If not, we need to concentrate on our original plan inside the safe Utopian areas. Matthew, Samantha, Eric, get those people converted to the Utopian way ASAP! I want everyone to have what we promised as soon as possible. While Jim's states continue to fight and struggle, I want our people to be safe and living the happy lives that we promised them. Giving them all 250 square feet in which to live, only working thirty-five hours a week, and everyone enjoying the same resources, everything! Do this successfully, and everything will work out. The capitalists will see how happy we are and quickly convert back to our society. I sincerely believe this, but I need everyone in this room to help make our country achieve the true Utopian Society we have promised and that the good citizens have voted for. We need to not fail them."

Back at the governor's mansion in Austin, Jacob and Jim are drinking coffee in Jim's office, trying to stay awake. Jacob is yawning as he speaks to Jim, "It's already 1 pm. We've been up over thirty hours.

Jim, who is looking like a mad scientist at this point, exclaims, "No time for sleep, Jacob! The calls keep coming in. Look at the map here!" Jim gets up and walks over to a US map on a giant touch screen on the wall. It has states in red symbolizing the United States, blue for Utopian, and torches in the states that are facing heavy riots, and a glowing radiation sign in Miami. He points from East to West as he says, "Look at this, Jacob. All these states have returned to the US: West Virginia, Nebraska, South Dakota, North Dakota, Wyoming, Montana, Idaho, Arizona, and Alaska have all joined us. That gives us twenty-five states!"

Jacob: "What about those torches in places like Atlanta and Denver, and a lot of Virginia and North Carolina?"

Jim: "Those are where the riots are the worst. Unfortunately, there are huge Utopian pockets in these places. We are in the process of having the National Guard ship those people out to the nearest Utopian territory. If they don't want to be here, I don't want them here. This land is free, for those who love the Constitution and who understand America's proud history. I think that by moving the Utopians out swiftly, we'll end the riots by the weekend, so we can start focusing on moving forward and reestablishing ourselves as the greatest country in the world. Hmm, look right here." He points to Utah and Colorado before continuing, "This is a problem. These Utopian states are right in our territory, but Utah should be coming back soon. Luke Montero, who was supposed to be Isaac's District Leader for that region, has been in constant contact with me. He wants to bring over Utah and rename it Deseret, and he wants to bring parts of other states with him."

Jacob: "I'm glad he wants to come over, but Deseret originally was going to be over 200,000 square miles and would include Nevada and Utah, with parts of a bunch of other states."

Jim gets a crazy look on his face and shouts, "That's it, the Utopians have Colorado, but we can annex it and combine it with Utah to form the new Deseret! We'll be up to twenty-six states and isolate the Utopians out of our area!" He points on the map at the line between red and blue states, "Let me call up our friend Luke right now." He runs over to his desk, grabs his phone, and quickly calls Luke."

Luke answers it asking, "Jim, do you have good news for me? Is Deseret back as it should be?"

Jim: "We've been over this ten times, Luke. Nevada is half Utopian and California isn't logical. However, Colorado is manageable, and, it's in the way. I don't know about you, but I would love to see it become part of the Free State of Deseret."

Luke: "Are you saying Utah can take over Colorado and combine with it to form Deseret? "

Jim: "That's *exactly* what I propose!"

Luke: "Not quite sure that's what the people wanted here, but it's a good compromise. I think I can sell this, but can we leave Nevada on the table?"

Jim: "I don't think, with what Las Vegas has become, that it should be part of Deseret, but as for the rest of the state, if we get it, it's yours!"

Luke: "Great!"

Jim: "I'll get with Maghee, and we'll do a conference call later. By tomorrow, Utah and Colorado will be Deseret, our twenty-sixth state, and you'll be their governor. I don't think Colorado will be that tough to take over, but Maghee is the expert. It was a very close election there, but for now, let's plan on noon tomorrow."

Luke: "Great, *finally* on Thursday, November 6th, 2036, the injustice of the past will be righted, and Deseret will take its place as a proud state of the FREE United States of America. Thank you, Jim, for finally making this happen!"

Jim: "Thank you, Luke Montero, for being a great patriot and going against Isaac. I know he offered you a lot of power."

Luke: "Freedom is what life is all about. I never was tempted."

Jim: "Thanks again, I look forward to working with you and will be in contact soon after I talk to Maghee." Jim hangs up.

Jacob: "This is really coming to together. Look at this map! We'll have contiguous borders. This is going better than I ever could have imagined."

Jim walks over to Jacob and sits down on a couch beside Jacob's chair saying, "Never give up on the American spirit, Jacob, NEVER! We have great resolve." As he is finishing speaking his phone rings. Jim answers, "Maghee, I was just talking about you."

Maghee: "I was just calling to let you know that North Carolina and Virginia's riots are under control, and with that being said, after looking at the map, I would like to request permission to unify our borders and take over Colorado."

Jim: "That's a perfect idea. Colorado is the only state in the middle of this. Utah is coming over, and Colorado is in the way. What I want to do is combine Colorado and Utah to form Deseret."

Maghee: "Deseret? Why?"

Jim: "Those people have longed for it, and their newspaper is even still called Deseret. Why not use this opportunity to right the former wrongs? It's a win-win. We take Colorado, it becomes Deseret, and we're unified."

Maghee: "Does that mean I have your permission to engage, sir?"

Jim: "Granted!"

Maghee: "Yes sir, thank you sir!"

Jim hears a click, and says in surprise, "He hung up on me. Ah well, no matter, this day just keeps getting better!"

Jacob: "I can't believe we're actually pulling this off!"

Jim: "It looks like our prayers have been answered. Anyways, Jacob, I think we should get some sleep. We've been up way too long."

Jacob get's up from his chair, "Good idea, I'm gonna go to the vice governor's quarters, and get some sleep."

Jim: "Ok, you go get some rest. I'm going to call Isaac and then crash here on the sofa." Jacob walks out of the room stretching and yawning, as Jim dials his cell phone.

Isaac, answers exclaiming, "Jim! I've been hoping to talk to you."

Jim: "I know, you've left me at least fifty messages since last night, but I've been pretty busy."

Isaac: "Yes, I can see that. Since we last spoke, you have influenced many states to secede and formed a new country. Why have you done this?! We had a gentleman's agreement that you were going to be in charge of my Southern Region, but instead, you started this secession for some reason. You need to reconsider what you're doing and stop this craziness. Come to Utopia, where you belong. You're causing a great deal of pain and suffering for everyone."

Jim: "What you need to understand, Isaac, is that you are the one causing great pain and suffering to the American people. This idea of a utopian society is wrong. It does not work when applied to humans. God has endowed us with the need for freedom, and when you take that freedom away, we become miserable, dead inside, and unable to function properly."

Isaac: "There you go again with your deity, making up things in your mind without facts to justify your actions. You are bringing the condemnation of the whole world upon yourself and those who follow you. We just had an emergency UN vote this past hour, in which all nations, except England, voted against your secession and your plans of nuking Miami."

Jim: "I don't care about the UN, Isaac. We plan on going isolationist."

Isaac: "Even Canada and Mexico voted against you! You need to realize that you're being blinded by your emotions and are acting irrationally, to the great detriment of everyone."

Jim: "We're following freedom, just as people have done for hundreds of years."

Isaac: "The American people freely voted for the Utopian government. You are going against your own Constitution and disobeying the will of the people you say you represent!"

Jim: "I don't think so. Most people want to be free – look at the country's votes. Nearly all of them voted against this. Only the Northeast and various big cities voted for this change."

Isaac: "Per the Constitution, Utopian Socialism would have received the majority of electoral votes and is the rightful government for all Americans. *You* are in violation of your own Constitution, which you hold sacred!"

Jim: "We are *upholding* the Constitution. Per the Declaration of Independence, upon which the US Constitution is largely based, we have freed ourselves from your regime. I'm sure you heard my speech. It is our *right*, it is our *duty*, to throw off such government and to establish new guards for our future security, which is what we have done."

Isaac: "Jim, you're not listening to reason, and the entire world has condemned you."

Jim: "I don't care about the entire world, I care about my country."

Isaac: "Thousands of Americans are being killed in riots caused by you." He shakes his head, as he tries to think of a way he can lure Jim back. Then he quickly says, "The blood of many Americans is on your hands!"

Jim: "Those deaths have happened because Americans want to maintain their freedom. They refuse to be oppressed by any government. These deaths are being caused by you! Anyone in our country who wants to be a Utopian is free to leave. As a matter of fact, I'm helping provide transportation for them to leave, so that they can join you."

Isaac: "What about New Mexico and your plans for Miami?!"

Jim: "I'm getting everyone out of Miami, so that not one person will be killed. As for New Mexico, they joined us readily, and we are transporting out all the people who want to be Utopians. Again, we've killed no one. Our hands are clean."

Isaac: "What is it going to take to bring you back into the Utopian Society?"

Jim: "NOTHING will make me leave this great country! We are free, and we are going to stay that way. If you choose to remain Utopian, that is your own problem and you're free to leave this land, but you will be considered our enemy, and we will never join you."

Isaac: "I can see your emotions are still too high to reason with you. Just, please, think about the UN condemnation. Think about what you've done and the pain you are bringing on the American people. You are taking away true happiness from these people just for your blind pursuit of freedom. Once again, you are a slave to the idea of freedom, and it is detrimental to everyone that follows you. You need to realize the error of your ways and come back to Utopia. Please think about all of this, Jim. I'll call you in a few days."

Jim: "I don't need to think it over! I *know* freedom is the answer. The only question is, do we accept your treasonous declaration of civil war and get those people out of there who long for freedom again?"

Isaac: "I was afraid that in your emotional state you might make more rash decisions. Therefore, I have contacted my ally, China. As we speak, they are sending troops to help us secure our borders to prevent an invasion by your forces. Rest assured that if you attack, China and I will defend."

Jim: "CHINA?! Have you lost your mind?! You're bringing in China? They have been working day and night for forty years, building bombs to destroy us! How could you possibly ever think of this? No good can come from it."

Isaac: "China is our friend, Jim. The only reason they have had to make bombs is to defend against people like you who threaten them."

Jim: "You're insane – turn this around right now! They should not be on American soil."

Isaac: "I need them to help me defend against you and what should be my military."

Jim: "China will steal your military secrets, then take you over, and after that, try to attack me."

Isaac: "They are my friends, Jim, and they are a peaceful people."

Jim: "I want them off this land!"

Isaac: "Then come back home and bring all the territories with you."

Jim: "Never!"

Isaac: "Then we have nothing further to discuss right now."

Jim hangs up and calls Maghee.

Maghee answers, "Maghee, here."

Jim: "Maghee, we have a dangerous situation developing. Isaac has called in the Chinese to secure his borders. I don't think anything will come of it, but I'm just giving you a heads up."

Maghee: "Do I have your permission to take any action necessary to secure our borders, sir?"

Jim: "Only if we're fired upon first! Got that? In the meantime, I'm calling it a day." Jim hangs up, tosses the phone onto a table next to the couch, rolls over, and covers himself up.

END CHAPTER

CHAPTER SIX

THE FAMILIES

Quite a lot is happening in America right now, wouldn't you say? Because of this, I'd like to pause our journey for a moment to show you how all this looks from the point of view of the two families talked about earlier, the Cordonia's and the Nolen's. Don't worry, we'll get right back to the main story soon. Let's start with the Cordonia's.

In Queens, New York, Eva Cordonia's mail has just arrived. She is coming inside after checking her mailbox. In her hand is an envelope from the federal government. When she gets inside, she sees her mother sitting in her chair knitting. Her mother asks, "That looks important. What does the letter say?" Eva opens up the envelope, pulls out a letter, and begins reading it silently. As she reads, her mother continues, "Don't keep me in suspense, Eva! What does it say?"

Eva has a large smile on her face as she exclaims, "This is great news, Mama: I'm going to be a nurse! It says I'm to attend a university right here in Queens to get a degree in nursing!"

Her mother stops knitting, gets up, and hugs her while exclaiming, "This is the best news I've ever heard – I love this country!"

Eva: "Czar Wolfe is really making great changes! For the first time ever, I'm hopeful for Teresa's future. It also says that you are to report to the principal of the elementary school after dropping off Teresa. They want you to be one of the cafeteria cooks."

Her mother: "Wonderful, we have a beautiful future ahead of us, with no worries about food or housing! No more working eighty hours a week! We have *truly* found Utopia."

Eva continues to read, stops, and flutters "Oh, oh, oh, it gets even better! It also says we're going to be moved into a thousand-square-foot apartment right by the campus. It even has three bedrooms!"

Eva's daughter Teresa, a five-year-old girl, comes in from another room and asks, "Mommy, Grandma, what are you so excited about?"

Eva picks her up and tells her, "Mommy is going to be a nurse! Now, you will have your own room, and you won't have to sleep on the floor in the living room anymore!"

Her daughter shouts, "I get my own room?"

Now that we know the Cordonia family is doing well, let's move on to the Nolen family, in Cincinnati, Ohio, to see how they're fairing.

That same evening, Brian is also coming inside his home after checking the mail. He, too, is holding an envelope from the federal government. He sits down at the kitchen table and opens it. After a few minutes, his wife Mary sits down beside him, looks at him as he is reading the letter, and says in a suspicious tone, "That looks important."

Brain replies, "It is. Here, read the top paragraph."

Mary takes it, and within five seconds, she shouts, "Oh, I can't believe this! They want us to go to Baltimore? BALTIMORE?!"

Brian sighs and replies, "It looks that way. The third paragraph says they want me to design a new mass transit system based on the train model. At least they are not separating *us*. They have you pegged as the Accounting Manager for this new transit company."

Mary quickly flips through the pages, asking, "What about George? Oh, here it is. It says they're sending him out to Stanford next year to learn agricultural engineering to help feed everybody."

George hears this from the living room and comes running in, yelling, "What!? I'm not going! I want to be a mechanical engineer, like Dad and Grandpa."

Mary puts her arm around him and says, "I'm sorry, George, but we don't have a choice in the matter. It's either we do what they tell us, or we will be forcibly sent to a 'reeducation center,' where they will brainwash us or drug us into submission!" As she says the term "reeducation center," she uses air quotes to emphasize her disdain for the Utopian government.

George: "Why do they have to send me all the way out to California and not a local college? Ohio has great farmland."

Brian: "I guess it's because they want California to be our agricultural territory now."

Mary: "One day in and I already hate this new government! I wish there was some way we could escape and start back over in the United States. All we'd have to do is make it over the bridge to Kentucky or swim across the river."

Brian: "You know they've been out there patrolling since Election Day, and they're sending everyone who tries to get away to those reeducation centers."

George: "I say we chance it, Dad. We can make it. We can go in the middle of the night, using our snorkeling gear."

Rick comes in from the living room, where he's been hiding, saying, "That's a good idea! We all got our certifications last year. We can do this!"

Brian: "It's too dangerous. If we get caught, we'll never be the same." He points to his head as he says, "They will take control of our minds."

George: "Maybe, but if we don't get caught, we will be free!"

Mary lets out a heavy sigh before saying, "Your dad's right. The risk is just too great."

Brian: "Besides, in another year, this utopian experiment may completely fail, and we will rejoin the United States. Before the Republican network started getting censored, it sounded like President Taylor was making great progress. He may even be able to free everyone by next year."

Rick: "You may be right, Dad. It sounded like President Taylor was taking back several states."

Mary: "I hope he is. Not only for our good, but for the rest of America, I hope this 'Utopia' doesn't last." She starts tidying up the room as she continues, "Well, it's getting late. I think we should all call it a night. That letter says we only have a few days to get ready to move."

Soon after everyone goes to bed, they all fall asleep, except for George. George is lying in his bed staring at the ceiling, planning his escape. He waits until 2 am to leave his room. Quietly, he sneaks out of his room, only to find his little brother standing in the hallway, and he is quickly greeted with the question, "What are you doing up, George?"

In a panic George gives a loud and sharp "Shhh!" hoping his parents won't wake up, before continuing speaking in a whisper, "I'm leaving. I'm going to cross the river down behind the old ball field we used to play in as kids."

Rick whispers back, "Where we used to fish, in that spot that nobody knows about?"

Both brothers tiptoe down the steps, and George continues, "Exactly, it's hidden. Only we knew the path, so it shouldn't be guarded. I can cross the river there and be free of this stupid government! I'm going to take some of the money we were planning to use to go to Italy. That ought to get me through until I can get a job."

Rick grabs his arm and says, "Hey, wait up! I'm going to go with you. They're liable to tell me I have to be a garbage man or something if I stay up here."

George: "I can't let you do that. It's too dangerous. Even though we're the only ones that knew that spot, who knows how heavily the water is guarded?"

Rick, talking in a regular voice, says, "If you don't take me, I'm going to go wake up Mom and Dad right now!"

George: "Why are little brothers always such a pain?"

"So, am I going?" Rick quickly replies.

George: "We could both die doing this, ya know."

Rick: "Better to be dead than to stay here!"

George sighs, and says, "Ok, let me add you to the note I wrote Mom and Dad." He pulls the note and a pen out of his pocket, scribbles on it and places it on the kitchen table, along with his cell phone, "Ok, go get dressed, and leave your cell phone in your room because if we take our phones, we'll be tracked and stopped. And BE QUIET! When you get back downstairs, we'll grab the gear from the garage, push the car down the street so it doesn't wake up Mom and Dad, and then, when it's out of range, start it up and be on our way to freedom."

Rick tiptoes back upstairs, goes into his closet, and rushes as quietly as he can back down the stairs, dressed. The brothers go to the garage, grab their scuba gear, and put it in the trunk, leaving the trunk open so as not to awaken their parents. Then they manually open the garage door. Afterwards, George puts the car in neutral and together, they push the car down the driveway and a short distance down the road. George closes the trunk as quietly as he can, and the duo gets in. George starts up the car, drives to the ball field and parks, and they get out of the car. Rick whispers, "It's still here!"

George whispers, "Yep, and let's hope we still remember the path!" They put on the scuba gear and grab flashlights. As they walk through the field, George continues, "We can't use these flashlights when we get close to the river."

Rick sees a couple of old trees he remembers and whispers, I know this path like the back of my hand!" He drops his flashlight, then says, "Follow me, and we'll be there in no time." They start walking down a path, through trees and rocks. Rick exclaims forgetting to whisper, "We're almost there, Brother!"

George sees a searchlight and excitedly whispers, "Shh! Get down, there's a searchlight!"

A confused Rick whispers, "What?" before being pushed to the ground by his brother. Rick gets angry for a second and asks "What was that all about!" George points to the light. Processing everything, Rick slowly says, "I thought for sure this area would be safe!"

George quickly yells in a whisper, "This is why I didn't want to bring you – why don't you go back home?" Guards see them and start chasing them from behind, shooting at them. Bullets are flying and hitting the trees behind them.

Rick runs towards the river, shouting, "Run for the water!" They both go running as fast as they can. As they are running, Rick gets shot in the knee. They both jump into the water and start swimming, diving deep underwater. Trying to avoid the bullets, they swim southward. George gets ahead of Rick, who can't go on and surfaces. Guards grab him as George continues on without knowing what's happened to Rick. George makes it to the other side, and gets out of the water.

He turns back and shouts, "I can't believe we made it, Rick!" Then he looks around for Rick. Moments later, a man who has been watching, walks up to him. George can't see clearly in the dark and asks, "Rick, is that you?"

The man heartily greets him, "Welcome to America, son! Glad you made it!"

George is in a panic and exclaims, "My brother! Have you seen my brother?"

"I'm sorry, son," says the man as he hands George a set of military binoculars. He continues, "Look over there" and points north.

George looks through the binoculars and sees Rick being carried away on a stretcher by Utopian guards. His leg is bleeding profusely. George starts yelling, "Rick, Rick! I've gotta go back!" He starts to jump in to the water, but man grabs him and stops him. He shouts "Let me go, I gotta save him!"

The man answers in a hopeless tone, "It's too late, son. They already have him. There's no saving him now."

George falls to his knees, crying, as he asks himself, "What have I done?"

A few hours pass. At the Nolen residence Mary and Brian are sound asleep in their bed, blissfully unaware of what has transpired overnight. They awaken to the sound of the doorbell followed by loud knocking. They both look at the clock on the wall that hangs above their bedroom door, which reads 6 am. With irritation in her voice Mary asks, "Who is that at *this* time of the morning?!"

Brian: "I don't know, honey, but at 6 am, I better go check it out." He gets up, puts a robe on, goes downstairs, and answers the door. He opens his door to find a police officer standing there and a government car is in his driveway. Very confused, he says, "Hello, officer, can I help you?"

The officer replies, "Brian Nolan?"

Brian, "Yes, sir, what can I do for you?"

Officer: "Do you know where your sons are right now, Mr. Nolen?"

Brian: Uh, my sons? They should be in bed asleep, like I was, until you came knocking on the door. Why?"

Mary, also still in pajamas and a robe, hurries down the steps and walks to the door. Seeing the officer outside, she asks, "What's going on?"

The officer sees her and asks, "Are you Mary Nolan?"

Mary replies with confusion, "Yes sir, can I help you?"

Officer: "As I just asked your husband, and I'm required to ask you as well, do you know where your sons are?"

Mary points up the stairs, as she says, "Upstairs sleeping, if you haven't already awakened them."

Officer: "So you know nothing about your sons' attempt to leave the country?"

Mary and Brian both emphatically shout, "What?!"

The officer pulls out a notepad and writes in it as he says, "Hmm, I see." He then whispers to himself, "Both parents deny involvement." Then he switches to a regular voice and addresses them again, "I've been sent here to inform you that your sons attempted to leave Utopia overnight.

George's whereabouts are unknown, and Rick has sustained a gunshot wound to the leg and is being treated at a hospital in Delhi. From there, he will be moved to the Cincinnati Reeducation Center."

Mary puts her hands up to her face in horror, and after a few seconds, she finds the strength to ask, "Is he alright?" After asking this, she goes to the closet to grab her jacket and purse.

The officer replies in a tone devoid of sympathy saying, "After he learns how to use his new knee, and after a few weeks of therapy in the reeducation center, he should be perfectly fine, and no, you cannot see him at this time, nor will you be allowed to see him anytime soon, not until his reeducation is complete."

Brian shakes his head and tries his best to mask his anger, then asks as politely as he can, "So, where did you say George is?"

Officer: "Far as we can tell, either he made it across the Ohio River, or he died on his fool's errand. His whereabouts are unknown at this time."

Sobbing and shaking Mary, asks, "When *can* we see Rick?"

Officer: "Your son's in good hands, Mrs. Nolen. Once he is completely reeducated, he will then be sent to your new residence in Baltimore."

Brian: "What about George?"

Officer: "We're searching the area for him. We will let you know if we find anything." He hands Brian a card, "Here's my card. If you hear from him, call me immediately. I must warn you, do not withhold information or you, too, will be taken to a reeducation center."

Mary: "Of course, Officer, just please, find my son."
The officer walks back to his car, reports in, and drives away.
Bryan and Mary immediately run up the stairs and check their
sons' rooms. Once they find that their rooms are empty, they
go back downstairs and find the note George left them.

A few hours later at the Nolen house, the home phone
rings. Mary and Brian both go running, and Mary gets there
first. Seeing the Hebron, Kentucky area code on the caller ID,
she quickly answers the phone and asks in a quivering voice,
"George, is that you?"

George replies, "Yeah, Mom, I made it across the Ohio
River!"

Mary puts the call on speaker phone and asks, "You're
ok?"

George: "Yeah, I am, but they got Rick. They shot
him in the leg and took him away. I didn't want him to go with
me, but he insisted. I thought he was right behind me, and I
didn't know until it was too late that he didn't make it. I'm so
sorry, Mom. I couldn't save him!"

Mary: "That's alright, George. The police came and
told us what happened. They took your brother to a hospital
and are going to send him to a reeducation center."

George: "Oh no, we've lost him, Mom! They'll drug
him into a zombie state and brainwash him."

Mary starts crying and says, "I know..."

Brian, in a very firm tone, tells George, "Listen very
carefully, George. Your brother is going to be ok. Everything
is going to be alright. At least you've made it to the United
States, so you can live your life freely. We will be ok over
here. Stay tough, alright?" Brian then grabs the phone from
Mary and hangs up. Then, the phone rings again. Brian yells,
"Don't answer it! I'm sure they're monitoring all our phone

calls. Anything we say can, and will, be held against us. We'll have to call from an encrypted phone, which is going to be really hard to get now."

Mary: "You're right. They have to be listening to our phone calls, but we'd better call that policeman soon. The longer we wait, the more they'll think we're withholding information."

Brian picks up the phone and calls the number on the officer's card. When the officer answers, Brian says, "Hello, Officer? This is Brian Nolan. You gave us instructions to call you if we heard from our son George. He just called us from the United States."

The officer very quickly asks, "Where?"

Brian replies, "He didn't tell me. Does it really matter? I told him we would be alright and to stay strong."

The officer makes a loud "Hmm" before asking, "You didn't try to convince him to come back?"

Brian: "No, I was just so happy to hear he was alive!"

Officer: "Very well, but if he calls back, be a good citizen and tell him to come home."

Brian says, "Yes, sir" before hanging up.

Once the call is ended, Mary asks, "What are we going to do?"

Brian shakes his head as he responds, "I don't know. I just don't know, but at least we know George is alive and free." They hug and cry…

END CHAPTER

CHAPTER SEVEN

THURSDAY

Back to the main story, it's now Thursday morning in Austin Texas, and Jim is sleeping on a couch in his headquarters. Jacob just got an urgent call from General Maghee, telling him that the Chinese are coming. Upon hearing this, he runs to Jim as quickly as he can and starts shaking him to wake him up. The moment Jim's eyes open Jacob greets him by shouting, "Wake up, wake up, Jim! Maghee is on the phone. He says it's urgent that he talks to you *now*!"

A not-quite-yet-cognitive Jim responds, "Huh, what?" He sits up, stretches, yawns, and blinks a few times before asking, "What time is it?"

With urgency in his voice, Jacob responds, "You've slept all night, it's 8 am, Thursday morning. Maghee says he really needs to talk to you," as Jacob hands Jim the phone.

In a serious tone Jim asks, "Hey Maghee, what's wrong?"

Straight to business, Maghee replies, "We've spotted multiple Chinese warships and several troop transports that are coming up from both sides of Costa Rica. We believe they are headed for New York and California. Looks like Wolfe's followed through with his plan to call in his friends. I would like to officially request permission to take out their satellites and destroy their ships before they reach American shores, sir, and I would suggest we consider attacking Costa Rica if they don't stop all ties with China."

Jim says his name like a cuss word, "Isaac?!" He turns toward Jacob, and tells him, "Isaac's gone ahead and called in the Chinese. He's afraid we're gonna attack him."

Jacob whispers to Jim, "You knew about this?"

Jim: "I just found out yesterday afternoon, but I fell asleep after being up for forty hours straight." He then hands the phone back to Jacob and has Jacob put it on speakerphone. "Maghee, I'm putting this on speaker so Jacob can hear what's going on."

Maghee completely ignores Jim's last statement and continues, "You're not going to let them onto American soil, are you, even if some parts of it are in the hands of the Utopians right now?"

Jim: "We don't need World War III right now."

Maghee: "Respectfully, sir, I believe it's already here. I suggest we knock out their satellites, including their nuclear defense shield, and we annihilate them."

Jim: "We can't do that. It would kill one quarter of the world's population. You know we don't work that way."

Maghee: *"Respectfully, sir,* it's either them or us. Once they are on our land, they won't stop. Ever since its founding, this has been a warring dynasty. I'm warning you, Jim. Do *not* overlook this threat. Please, let me save us while we still have the chance!"

Jim: "No, we cannot start a war. If they are foolish enough to attack us, then we can finish it, but we do not start wars. That has never been our way."

Maghee: "So, we just let the ships land and let them put their military on American soil?!"

Jim: "It's Utopian soil for now. We will deal with getting them out in due time."

Maghee: "Alright Jim, you're the Commander-in-Chief. If your orders are that they have to throw the first punch, despite my reservations, I'll abide by it. That said, if you don't object, I'm going to start preparing for the worst and build heavy fortifications on our borders. Now, what do you want to do about Costa Rica and any other Latin American countries that allow Chinese troops in our hemisphere?"

Jim: "Mexico, I intend to ally with, and after everything settles down, we'll deal with these other countries and China, and they *will* leave. Make no mistake about that."

Maghee: "Very well, but may the record show, it was my belief that we should have taken them out, today, while we still could. That said, every moment we wait is another moment they're building up, and every hour that passes increases the projected number of casualties, *when* this turns into an armed conflict."

Jim: "Understood, but not now. How is everything else going?"

Maghee: "Not bad, all of our states are secure, and the riots are way down. I think we're in good shape. Just about everyone who wants to be Utopian is either out or is on a list to be shipped out."

"Great, I'm going to call Mexico and Canada and see if we can't get them onboard with us. Keep up the good work, Maghee," Jim says right before he hangs up.

Jacob: "Maghee may be right. China is a huge force, and their history always suggests war."

Jim: "I know, and I will deal with it as early as next month."

Jacob, ever the pessimist, replies, "Good, glad to hear that; I just hope it won't be too late!"

Jim gets up shaking his head and starts walking away, saying, "Now to go get ready to face the day, and then I'll deal with our neighbors."

A little while later, Jim walks into his office and sits down at his desk. Jacob has been in the room working on a laptop, pouring over all the events since Tuesday and working on budgets. Jim says to him, "Now, to call Mexico and then, Canada."

Jacob: "Here's hoping this goes well. It'd be nice if at least one of our neighbors didn't hate us."

Jim: "I've got a good feeling about Mexico."

Jacob: "You have a good feeling about Mexico, after they voted in the UN to *condemn* us?!"

Jim: "I know it doesn't seem good right now, but I've had a great relationship with President Rodriguez throughout my time as governor, and at their core the people of Mexico believe in freedom. I think we have a friend in them."

Jacob: "I hope you're right, Jim."

Jim: "Well, let's find out." He opens one of his desk drawers, which contains a big book with the phone numbers of various international leaders. He grabs the book and finds "Mexico (United Mexican States)." He then calls President Rodriguez of Mexico, using the landline phone on the desk. When President Rodriguez picks up, Jim says, "Hola, Presidente! This is Jim Taylor. Como esta?"

A cautious President Rodriguez answers, "Senor Taylor, I don't know yet, how are you?"

Jim, with air of optimism, replies, "Well, my fellow Capitalist, you tell me."

"What do you mean?" asks a confused President Rodriguez.

Jim: "I understand you voted to condemn my country for the plans to nuke Miami tomorrow at noon."

President Rodriguez: "Si, Senor Taylor, bombing Miami is unacceptable! If you nuke Miami, the next thing I know, you're nuking me. Despite our years of friendship, I'm worried you may become another Hitler and will start taking countries over, one by one."

Jim: "I'm giving everyone a chance to get out. I don't want to do it, but I cannot have hostile elements in strategic parts of my country. The Gulf of Mexico must remain protected."

President Rodriguez: "What about me? My country uses the Gulf of Mexico, extensively."

Jim: "The use of the Gulf of Mexico is for the United States and its allies. If you are my ally, then you will be allowed to use the Gulf, but any hostile intrusion into those waters will be met with swift and brutal retaliation."

President Rodriguez: "Jim, my friend, I am afraid you've gone mad – you've become mad with power! Am I going to have to degrade myself like that pseudo-communist Wolfe and ask China to bolster my defense?"

Jim: "Mr. President, you and I share a love of freedom. Our nations are both Democracies. Isaac's Utopian Socialism is, indeed, Communism. All great historians have predicted the move from Socialism to Communism – just look to Karl Marx and Friedrich Engels. It's inevitable. That's why I'm calling to ask, are you going to side with Isaac and China, who *are* Communists, or are you going to side with freedom?"

President Rodriguez: "I'm afraid it's not that cut and dry."

Jim: "It is to me, do you want to be free, yes or no? It's that simple."

President Rodriguez: "Of course, I and my people want to be free."

Jim: "Then, please, become my ally and help us fight against the tyrannical governments of Communism."

President Rodriguez: "This all sounds good, but how can I trust you?"

Jim: "You already *know* you can trust me, because, if I was really a war monger, I would have taken you over already, started a nuclear war with China, and the Utopian States would have been invaded. I simply want freedom, and I want you to help me fight for freedom and stop this Communist infestation. And besides that, in the past, did I ever do one thing to hurt you? Have I done one thing to dishonor your people? I'm telling you, Rodriguez, we are the last hope for the world. If not us, then who will fight for freedom?"

President Rodriguez lets out a heavy sigh and answers, "You are right, amigo. I wish this were not happening, but you are right. If freedom dies, it dies with us. 'Viva la America y muera el mal gobierno!'"

Jim: "Viva la Libertad!"

President Rodriguez: "Viva!"

Jim: "Welcome aboard, my friend! I trust you'll inform the UN of your reversal?"

President Rodriguez: "Of course, Jim. Is there anything else I can do to help stop the spread of this infectious plague known as Communism?"

Jim: "Not that I can think of right now. I'll have General Maghee contact your top generals to fill you in on what's happening and see if there is anything you can do to help."

President Rodriguez: "Bueno, and I assume Mexico is free to use the Gulf?"

Jim: "Of course it is, of course you are! We take care of our friends. Glad to have you on board, and thank you."

President Rodriguez: "Of course, Presidente, and I'll get right with my generals and diplomats and apprise them of our new relationship."

"Excellent, and I'll do the same! Talk to you later," Jim says as he hangs up the phone. He then shouts jubilantly, "Yes, we've got an alliance with Mexico! Long live Liberty – Viva la Libertad! Jacob, drop everything and tell Maghee to contact their generals, and tell our diplomats we're friends."

Jacob looks up from his laptop and says in a surprised tone, "What, we got Mexico, how?" He shakes his head and then continues, "Okay, right away, Jim!" Jacob then jumps up and runs out of the room.

Jim then goes back to his book and finds "Canada (Dominion of Canada)" and dials the number for Prime Minister Tremblay. When Prime Minister Tremblay answers, Jim heartily greets him saying, "Prime Minister Tremblay, this is Jim Taylor. How are you today, sir?"

With a thick air of suspicion in his voice, Prime Minister Tremblay replies, "I'm ok, Mr. Taylor, what about you?"

In an attempt to remedy the Prime Minister's obvious tension, Jim asks him, "Please, call me Jim."

To which Prime Minister Tremblay fakes a chuckle and says in a forced, almost passive aggressive demeanor "Alright. Jim. What can I do for you?"

Jim: "I understand that you voted to condemn my country for a necessary action I must take tomorrow to secure internal peace."

With anger in his voice, Prime Minister Tremblay replies, "An *action*?! You plan on *nuking* one of your own cities! That is something I and the people of Canada simply cannot support!"

Remaining calm, Jim says, "I don't want to do this, but I have no choice. Besides, everyone will be evacuated, so there will be no loss of life."

Now even angrier, Prime Minister Tremblay replies, "No loss of life?! What about the wildlife and the damage to the environment? Not to mention the fact that you seceded from your own country!"

Jim: "The Utopians separated from the USA. They discarded the Constitution and became Socialists, forming a new country altogether. For the loss of wildlife and the minor environmental problems that will come from the nuclear fallout, I am sorry, but the greater good is at stake."

Prime Minister Tremblay: "I simply cannot support you, and I personally plead with you to stop this madness! Do not do this to Miami. Obey your countrymen's wishes and rejoin the Utopians."

Jim: "I cannot do that. They have left the country on their own, and because of them, Miami has to go."

Prime Minister Tremblay, seeing that his anger isn't working, switches his tone from one of anger to a professorial, almost condescending tone, saying, "You will be sorry if you go ahead with your plans. You will be condemned by the entire world, and we will support full economic sanctioning against you. After all, we have been moving towards socialism for decades, as it is the *better* way. We are prepared to join Czar Wolfe, and we will vote on this in the next election. We, too, will become a utopian socialist nation. Jim, please, join with us, and let your people live a worry-free life."

A switch suddenly flips on in Jim's mind. Though he now considers Canada an enemy, he remains calm as he says, "Ok, Mr. Tremblay, if that's the way you want it, you are no longer an ally of the US. All intrusions into our borders, including the Great Lakes, will be met with swift military action."

Reverting back to anger, Prime Minister Tremblay replies, "You can't do that. We use the Great Lakes for trade. We have several ports there, not to mention, they are part of our water supply."

Jim coldly says, "Not anymore, so I suggest you evacuate those ports, as they will be destroyed seventy-two hours from now, along with any Canadian vessels in the Great Lakes. Consider this an official warning. In seventy-two hours, you must evacuate the Great Lakes or any Canadian incursion vessels will be destroyed, and their presence will be considered an act of war."

Prime Minister Tremblay: "You wouldn't!"

Jim: "I will, and this is your final warning. You have a seventy-two-hour window to get your citizens out of those ports and recall all your ships from the Great Lakes. The order will be given Sunday at noon."

Prime Minister Tremblay: "You are a mad man!"

Jim: "I am fighting for freedom, and I had hoped you would want to join me. I was unaware that you were planning to completely convert to socialism. I am very disappointed to hear that, and I am sorry for the sake of your people. Seventy-two hours." Jim then hangs up and starts thinking.

While Jim is busy making calls, Isaac's district leader from Philadelphia Alfred Schmidt is doing a little diplomacy of his own, inside an office building in downtown Detroit. He is in a rectangular windowless conference room. On the end wall hangs an American flag that covers the entire wall, and the other walls are a dark gray color. In the center of the room is a conference table. Alfred is at the end wall pacing, waiting for his two guests to arrive. After a few minutes of pacing, the door opens and both guests come in together. Terrell Bone, the Utopian District Leader reassigned to Chicago, and Frank Barker, the Utopian District Leader of Detroit both sit down, and Alfred goes to the edge of the table and starts speaking in his usual quick, quirky manor. "Thanks for agreeing to meet me here in Detroit. To say the least, this is a troubling time. We all know Isaac Wolfe is *not* the man to lead us out of our current crisis. We are losing territory day by day. China is learning all of our military secrets, while our own military has no direction. Our workers are becoming lazy, just when we need to have people working harder to rebuild our weapon supply. We *must* fight Jim Taylor and his merry band of traitors and take back *our* land."

After a short moment of silence, Frank Barker responds, "You are completely right, but Wolfe isn't budging. I see no way he tries anything other than a diplomatic solution."

Immediately, Terrell Bone chimes in, "Wolfe is way too closed-minded, but what can we do, Alfred? He's the leader of our government."

Alfred Schmidt leans in on the table and says with wide eyes, "Well, I have an idea."

Frank Barker leans in and says, "Please, enlighten us."

Alfred Schmidt: "Isaac Wolfe must go." He pounds his fist on the table and continues, "We *must* remove him from power! I can take over once that is done."

Somewhat in disbelief Frank Barker asks: "And how are you going to do that? How do you take down a Czar? He's been voted in as 'Czar for life.'"

Alfred Schmidt quickly replies, "I have a plan to remove him. Don't worry about that."

"But how?" asks Terrell Bone.

Alfred Schmidt: "I have a fail-proof plan. You don't need to worry about it. What you do need to worry about is supporting the fact that Wolfe must go. There is no other way, as he is simply incapable and incompetent. He has a false understanding of life, which makes him unfit to rule. Every minute that he rules this land is a minute closer to us being completely overtaken by either Taylor or China!"

Frank Barker: "Even if we somehow remove Wolfe, how would we ensure that you can take over?"

Alfred Schmidt: "That is why I am here. If I can gain your support and the support of all the District Managers, then I can execute my plan to remove him and take over with full support of the existing government. That way, the people will have no choice but to accept my regime, and we will institute a more perfect government, one in which we will become a world power."

Terrell Bone mumbles, "Wolfe is such a nice guy, though."

Alfred Schmidt then yells, "And so, you would let a nice guy ruin our country and by his ineptitude cause you to be enslaved by Taylor or the Chinese? Is that what you want for yourself and your family?"

Terrell Bone firmly responds, "No, no I don't."

Alfred Schmidt: "Then, join me, and together we can pave the path to a bright future. The first step is here in this

room. I implore you. Will you join me and help save this
country, or will you cower and, through inaction, see to its
end?"

Frank Barker: "I'll join you. Come on, Terrell. Look,
you've lost your St. Louis Region, and soon, you'll lose
Chicago. Most of Illinois is in an uproar. We have to stop
Taylor's momentum before he overtakes us completely."

Terrell Bone: "Ok, I'm in."

Alfred Schmidt: "Then I can count on your support?"

Terrell Bone: "Yes, I'm in."

Alfred Schmidt: "Very good, you will *not* be sorry."

Frank Barker: "But, what about the others? Most of
them are clearly going along with Wolfe and are as blind as he
is, believing in a diplomatic solution."

Alfred Schmidt: "I will explain to them the dire
situation that Wolfe has thrown our innocent country into and
bring up the riots they are having in their Districts. I believe I
can gain most, if not all, of their support in the next month. It's
only going to get worse, and they will become desperate. Then,
they will understand that they have to help make the change.
They will join us, and we will defeat Taylor, kick China out,
and take our rightful spot back as the sole world power."

That afternoon, a large Russian fleet composed of many battleships, destroyers, aircraft carriers, troop transport ships, and submarines come to the shores of Alaska on a mission of conquest. The weather was nice, the temperature nearly forty degrees. It was a sunny day.

Thousands of Russian planes, almost like a swarm, blacken the sky. They start shooting down all non Russian planes, be they military or civilian. Within minutes the Alaskan military meets them, and while their air force shoots down many Russian planes and their navy sinks many Russian ships, the Russian numbers are just far too overwhelming. Eventually, the Russians gain air superiority and their bombers sink the ships of the Alaskan fleet.

Not long after this, the Russians begin a heavy bombardment, using bombers, the guns from their ships, and missiles from their submarines.

Soon, troops come to land. Some land boats directly on the shore, tanks leading the charge, and others are air-dropped, parachuting out of planes. While these, too, are met with a valiant resistance, the Russian numbers are just too great...

In only a few short hours the cities of Petersburg, Juneau, Ketchikan, Homer, Seward, Tok, Anchorage, Kenai, Valdez, Nome and St. Paul, along with the air stations at Kodiak, Sitka and Cordova, all fall.

A Russian General, Igor, who is a moderately obese man about the age of 55, with gray receding hair and an eye patch over his right eye, walks triumphantly along the streets of downtown Juneau, Alaska. He is closely followed by an entourage of soldiers. With celebration in his voice, he orders his men to take down the American flag and to replace it with a Russian flag. As his troops gleefully replace the flag, he calls the Kremlin. Speaking in Russian he says proudly, "Sir, we have retaken Alaska!"

With joy in his voice Russian President Baskov replies, "Very good, comrade! Was there much loss of life, Igor?"

General Igor: "Easy victory, they were completely caught off guard. We destroyed all of their naval and air force vessels. We are completely secure."

President Baskov: "Finally, we have rightfully reclaimed our land that the Americans stole from us over 170 years ago."

General Igor: "This is a great day in Russia history, sir. You are now a legend."

President Baskov: "Good work, keep it secure!" He then hangs up.

Back at the Austin headquarters, Jim is in an office furnished with a red couch and a wooden desk with a landline phone on it. There is a giant map of North America on the end wall opposite the couch. Jim is standing next to the wall looking at the map. Jacob runs into the office and shouting, General Maghee is calling. He said the Russians are attacking and he needs to talk to you on a landline right now!"

"The Russians are attacking? The US?" Jim asks in a skeptical tone, before walking to the desk. Once there, he quickly picks up the phone, calls General Maghee, and says, "Maghee, what's going on?"

In a serious tone General Maghee replies, "Sir, the Russians have entered American soil."

Not understanding yet what's happened, Jim asks, "What? Isaac invited Russia in with China?"

General Maghee: "No sir, Alaska has fallen to Russia in a surprise attack!"

Jim: "What?! What about the Alaskan Command? Couldn't they defend?"

General Maghee: "They fought valiantly, sir, but they were outnumbered, twenty to one."

Jim: "Did you see any hints of this coming? How could you *not* have Alaska protected?"

General Maghee: "We're simply spread too thin, sir, trying to protect all the states that have just been freed, along with the threat of China, and the Utopian central government. We only have so many resources, but with Isaac's decline in military spending, we just don't have much."

Jim, in a frustrated, angry tone asks, "Are you saying you can't get it back?"

General Maghee: "Not without risking losing the states we have. We just don't have that kind of manpower."

Jim gets a fire in his eyes as he says, "No, that's not good enough!"

General Maghee: "Look, Jim, we just can't. If you would have let me take out the Russian and Chinese satellites earlier this week, we wouldn't be having this conversation. I don't make recommendations lightly."

Jim: "Well, sorry, General, but we don't start wars. However, Russia has now started something, and I plan to finish it. Take out their satellites!"

General Maghee: "I can do that, sir, but it doesn't free Alaska.

Jim: "No, it doesn't, but it makes what I'm about to do a lot easier."

General Maghee: "And what would that be, sir?"

Jim: "I want you to take out all of their satellites, but leave up their direct communication link. I want to be able to continue to talk to Baskov."

General Maghee: "Yes sir, but we don't have enough resources to start a major bombing campaign."

Jim: "That's not what I have in mind. Just do what I say. I'll call you back after I talk to President Baskov. When will their satellites be destroyed?"

General Maghee: "Within thirty minutes sir."

Jim: "Perfect! Talk to you soon." He hangs up, walks into an office, and picks up another phone and starts dialing.

President Baskov, seeing an American area code, answers the phone saying, "Hello, Isaac, my friend!"

An aggravated Jim responds in an angry but still civil tone saying, "No, President Baskov, this is Jim Taylor, President of the United States of America. I've noticed your recent attack on my state."

President Baskov scoffs before asking, "Are you referring to Alaska?"

Jim: "Yes, that's the one."

President Baskov: "Hmmm I see, and what does that have to do with you? It should be Czar Wolfe's concern, not yours."

Jim: "Alaska has been a US state since 1959, and their Governor announced yesterday that they would not be joining Utopia but would instead, remain one of the United States. Therefore, by attacking the State of Alaska, you have just declared war on the United States of America."

President Baskov: "We are only taking back what you stole from us almost 170 years ago."

Jim: "Stole?! We bought that land, fair and square. You were looking to sell."

President Baskov: "Yes, but we only sold you the land because your motherland, England, was going to seize it and take it from us. Your kind has always been war mongering and territorially expansive."

Jim: "Uh-huh, and your history is any better? Peter the Great conquered and took over other nations to build your empire back in the late 1600s."

President Baskov: "What do you wish to accomplish with this phone call? We have simply reclaimed our territory that you took from us under coercion."

Jim: "Look, Baskov, I'm getting my state back. Now, do we do this the easy way, or do you suffer in the process?"

President Baskov: "Alaska is Russia's, and we will not lose it a second time."

Jim: "You sure? As you can probably see, your satellites are going out one by one."

President Baskov: "What?"

Jim: "Yep! Seeing as how you declared war, I'm taking the necessary steps to win. I've ordered all of your satellites to be destroyed, except the direct-link satellite, so that we can continue to communicate."

President Baskov: "You don't have that type of technology."

Jim: "Check your radar. I'll hold." Jim drums his fingers on the desk while he's waiting

President Baskov puts Jim on hold, sets his phone down, and tells his young aide Ivan, who is sitting next to him, "Ivan, get Tarasov on the phone, I want to confirm something." Ivan dials his phone and hands it to President Baskov. President Baskov immediately asks, "Tarasov, are our satellites functioning?"

Tarasov replies, "I was just about to call, sir. I'm not sure what's happening, but our satellites are going out one by one! I have no idea what's happening, and I see no way to stop it."

President Baskov hangs up on Tarasov and picks up his phone, and takes Jim off hold and shouts, "What have you done?!"

Jim: "I just told you. I've destroyed your satellites, and now, you are blind. My next step is the nuclear destruction of your country, city by city, if all of your troops are not out of Alaska by 1 pm Central Standard Time tomorrow. With an eight-hour difference, that should be 9 pm your time. At that time I will authorize the destruction of your cities, one by one, every hour, on the hour: 1 pm will be Kazan; 2 pm will be Kiev; 3 pm will be Moscow. After that, if you still have not surrendered Alaska, I will just nuke the rest of your country. Alaska will be mine by 5 pm tomorrow, one way or another. Don't bother to retaliate because our nuclear defense shield is up and fully operational."

President Baskov: "You won't do that! The world will condemn you."

Jim: "You and the UN have already denounced me, but that is not a deterrent, President Baskov. You see, in both world wars, America stood up for the world and fought for freedom. I'm simply doing the same thing here."

President Baskov: "You won't kill over a hundred million people!"

Jim: "In the name of Freedom, I will! You have until 1 pm tomorrow. My advice is, you start evacuating now." Jim hangs up.

Dumbfounded, President Baskov tells Ivan, "Get my advisors together, and tell them what's happened. We need to have an emergency meeting." With a look of panic on his face, Ivan runs out of the room.

About half an hour later, President Baskov is sitting at a table in the Kremlin, surrounded by his advisors.

Advisor to President Baskov and General Roshenko starts by saying, "Sir, we must consider this a real threat!"

Baskov: "I just don't see how he would do this. No one would completely annihilate another country!"

His second advisor and former diplomat Sasha Malinov says, "I agree, he's bluffing."

His third advisor Fyodor Averin asks, "But what if he's not? He will nuke Kazan at 9 pm tomorrow, and over a million will die."

President Baskov: "He won't do it!"

General Roshenko: "He might sir. Look at his strategy. It's how the US operates. They start small and work their way up. Kazan's population is 1.1 million, Kiev's population, 2.7 million, and then, here in Moscow, 12 million. He will nuke Kazan first to show he is serious, and then he will follow through with the rest."

President Baskov: "If he does, what can we do stop him or retaliate?"

General Roshenko: "Unfortunately, there is no getting through his nuclear defense shield. He has knocked out our satellites, which has stopped military communication. Attacking Texas would be impossible now. He would stop us before we got there. We have no options."

President Baskov slams his fist down on the table and then shouts, "We are Russia! We, too, have options."

Fyodor Averin: "We could nuke England, hit their motherland."

President Baskov: "Excellent idea, we threaten to nuke England if he nukes Kazan! I see no way he will use his nukes then. I'll call him now."

President Baskov picks up his phone and calls Jim Taylor. Jim answers, asking, "President Baskov, are you calling to inform me you are withdrawing from Alaska?"

President Baskov replies, "I have no intentions of doing that, but if you nuke Kazan at 1 pm, we will nuke England at 1:01 pm!"

Jim: "Then, I will order the nuclear destruction of your entire country at 1:02 pm. I protect my friends."

President Baskov: "Quite the contrary, you are putting your friends in grave danger. You would not want to see any harm come to them, now would you?"

Jim: "You don't understand freedom or have any clue as to what it means. It is better to be dead than to not be free."

President Baskov: "You are right. I do not understand, but we are not leaving Alaska. You do not understand how freedom has destroyed our country. Your President Reagan forced us into Democracy. Then, your country left us to the dogs. You are the evil empire, and we will not be bullied anymore." He shouts, "Alaska is ours!" and hangs up.

Sasha Malinov asks, "What if he nukes Kazan tomorrow?"

President Baskov: "He won't, he's bluffing."

Sasha Malinov looks down and says, "I sure hope so…"

Also that afternoon, Isaac Wolfe receives several worried calls from his district leaders, so he calls for a six o'clock open forum meeting that night, to be held in Washington, D.C. Isaac begins the meeting by saying, "Thank you all for coming. Today, several of you have reached out to me asking for a meeting, so the floor is yours. What's on your minds?"

The second Isaac stops talking, Philadelphia District Leader Alfred Schmidt stands up and says, "Sir, we are very concerned about the recent expansion by Jim Taylor. We have already lost over half of our land, plus we now have China learning all of our military secrets. We *must* put a stop to both of these situations at once!"

With a calm demeanor, Isaac responds, "As we discussed *just* the other day, everything is under control. We simply need to stay the course. China will only be here for a little while. Soon Jim Taylor's momentum will start to die, and we will stabilize. Rest assured, everyone, all is well. The people are happy, and they are adjusting well to Utopian Society. Sure, there are some misguided rebels calling themselves freedom fighters, but the reeducation centers are dealing with them, enlightening them. Within a year, all of the protesters will be reeducated. Remember, Rome wasn't built in a day. We have to be patient and stay the course. This is working. Once we have a complete Utopian Society in our Territories, it will start to spread to even the most rebellious. Eventually, states will start coming back to us, one by one. Everything is under control, and there is nothing to worry about. I want to reiterate, China is only protecting our borders, and we are reeducating those who need it. Utopian Society is starting to thrive in many areas, but we have to stay the course."

Still standing, District Leader Alfred Schmidt shouts, "No, sir – we *have* to defend ourselves! China is a threat, ready to take us over, and you are enabling them! Taylor is not going to stop until he takes us over. He already said he is going to nuke Miami tomorrow! He is a mad man and *must be killed!*"

District Leader Frank Barker quickly chimes in, "I agree, Taylor needs to be stopped, and China needs to go."

District Leader Terrell Bone: "I agree also."

District Leader Jerrod Michaelson: "I agree. My constituents in the New England area are very nervous about China. Taylor and China, both, need to go."

Secretary of the Treasury Eric Masterson: "We have to stop Taylor. He has to go. Isaac, we can't wait for the momentum to stop. On the contrary, *we* have to stop it. Other Territories are in danger of converting, and we're going to run out of money to run our country."

Secretary of Labor Matthew Roberts: "We're losing key people in the labor force, as the reeducation centers take time. We need good, qualified managers to run our operations, or we're going to have severe food shortages."

Isaac: "No we won't. Our Brazilian neighbors have agreed to share their food with us. We will not go hungry. We *are* winning this war. I know we are losing battles, but we are winning this war."

Secretary of Homeland Security Pablo Martinez: "How can you say that? Our defense is weak, and we are in serious trouble! Both Taylor and China could take us over at any time."

District Leader Alfred Schmidt: "Exactly! That's why we need to build up our military immediately, working around the clock to build weapons necessary to defend our borders and take out Taylor."

Secretary of Homeland Security Pablo Martinez: "I agree with Schmidt. We need to do this."

Secretary of Labor Matthew Roberts: "Yes, we *have* to do this."

Isaac: "So, what are you suggesting, we build up our military and then attack Jim Taylor?"

District Leader Alfred Schmidt: "YES! We build up our forces in the next three months. We kick out China and use Special Forces to take out Taylor. Then, one by one, we start taking back over those people and lands we have lost to him."

Secretary of Homeland Security Pablo Martinez: "Valid plan."

District Leader Frank Barker: "I agree."

District Leader Terrell Bone: "I agree."

Secretary of Labor Matthew Roberts: "I agree."

Secretary of the Treasury Eric Masterson: "I'm for all of this!"

District Leader Jerrod Michaelson: "Me too."

District Leader Tom Rhodes: "No, this is the 21st century. Military is no longer a need. Instead, we need to find diplomatic solutions."

District Leader Tony Sanchez: "I agree with Tom."

District Leader Henry Pilot: "We can solve this peaceably."

District Leader Richard Jackson: "I've been bouncing back and forth, but we are struggling in New York. I think Schmidt is right. We have to stop this. There is no reason why we can't utilize the Miami citizens who are coming to New York to start building weapons around the clock."

Isaac: "So, I can see there is dissension among us. Let us have a vote. Who is for holding the course, and who is for the barbaric act Schmidt is proposing? We'll go with District Managers first, then my cabinet." Isaac then points to them, one by one, saying their name and which plan they are for.

The District Leader Vote goes as follows:

Tom – Isaac

Jerrod – Schmidt

Richard – Schmidt

Frank – Schmidt

Terrell – Schmidt

Tony – Isaac

Henry – Isaac

Schmidt sarcastically, with a bow and arms spread, says "No question here!" when asked.

Somewhat in shock, Isaac mumbles, "So, out of my eight District Leaders, five are going with Schmidt, ok…" He then takes a vote from his cabinet members, which goes as follows:

Secretary of the Treasury Eric Masterson: "100% Schmidt."

Secretary of Housing Samantha Jones: "I'm with you, Isaac, you know that."

Secretary of Homeland Security Pablo Martinez: "I love you, Isaac -- like a brother, but Schmidt is right."

Secretary of Labor Matthew Roberts: "Schmidt."

In disbelief Isaac exclaims, "So, my own cabinet is also against me, by a 3-1 vote!"

District Leader Alfred Schmidt: "That makes it 8-4, a clear mandate. Isaac, you need to listen to us."

Isaac firmly says, "We are not changing course; the eight of you need to think this through! We have worked very hard to get to this day, and we're not going to ruin it. We have the beginnings of a complete Utopian Society. We will not let our citizens down. We will not let the world down. The realization of the world's dream of a complete Utopia is not that far away, a perfect world for our children, and our children's children. I will not let that opportunity die. We *will* stay the course, and we will be victorious."

District Leader Alfred Schmidt yells, "Isaac, you are killing us! There will be no future, as our country will be gone. You are aiding China and Taylor, while you are forcing us to destroy ourselves. If this does not stop now, there will be nothing left of us, nothing to leave for our children and our children's children, *nothing*! You are destroying us and our future. You *must* change your mind and take our advice." He shakes his head, then continues his barrage, "I mean, look, your own cabinet is 3-1 against you! Surely, you can't be so blind as to overlook this clear a majority. You have to know you are thinking wrong."

Isaac: "You and the others are being led by emotion. You see the terrible events, the temporary decline, and you are reacting emotionally. You need to step back and look at this objectively, with the big picture in mind. We *are* winning this war. Long term, we are the victors. We just need to ride out the storm. I'm telling you, all is good."

District Leader Alfred Schmidt yells, "*You* are blind. Soon it will be all twelve of us telling you that you are wrong, and what then?"

Isaac: "Even *if* that happens, we will still stay the course. We are on an historic run, Utopia for all. I will not let it die. We are here, and it will be done. It's getting late, and it would do everyone good to get some sleep and to think this through. Good night, everyone." He gets up and leaves the room, ending the meeting.

END CHAPTER

CHAPTER EIGHT

ELECTION WEEK WRAP-UP

The next morning President Jim Taylor and Vice President Jacob Neilsen are sitting at a coffee table at their headquarters. There is a briefcase sitting next to Jim's leg. In front of them is a wall-mounted TV, tuned in to a news channel. Jacob asks Jim, "It's a few minutes before noon; are you going ahead as planned with the nuclear destruction of Miami, or have you changed your mind?"

Jim replies, "Everyone has been evacuated, so we are clear to go."

A hesitant Jacob asks, "But if everyone is gone, why do you have to do this?"

Jim: "We've been through this before, Jacob. There are two reasons for doing this."

Jacob: "Two?"

Jim: "Yes, reason number one is that, as long as Miami remains an option, socialists will flock to it. In order to safeguard freedom, we need to guard against communism. Reason number two, we need to show the world that we still have nuclear capabilities and are serious about using them if the need arises." A few moments later Jim's phone rings. Jim answers it and says, "Maghee, right on time."

General Maghee asks, "Do I have the go ahead, sir?"

Jim puts the briefcase on the table and opens it. Inside is an elaborate keyboard and several other buttons all attached to a circuit board, welded to the inside of the briefcase. Jim starts typing and hitting buttons, as he says to General Maghee, "I'm just punching in the code now. Please punch yours in."

General Maghee also has a briefcase similar to Jim's. He, too, presses buttons and then says, "Done."

A red button starts to flash in Jim's briefcase. He tells Maghee, "Ok, I'm launching now" as he presses the flashing red button. He then continues, "In fifteen minutes, Miami will be only a memory." Jim and Jacob stand next to the window and look out. They see two large ICBMs launching into the Texas sky from a nearby base. A stunned Jacob looks at the TV and sees that the launch is being televised. Jim comments, "I've authorized this to be broadcast to the world."

An excited TV newscaster exclaims, "This is historic, ladies and gentleman! Two Inter Continental Ballistic Missiles are headed to the city of Miami and are expected to reach the city in five minutes. They will completely obliterate the area for years to come!"

Meanwhile in Russia, President Baskov and his advisors are watching this event on television as well. The former diplomat Sasha Malinov exclaims, "He's actually doing it, he's nuking Miami!"

Fyodor Averin: "He will surely nuke us if he's doing this to his own city!"

President Baskov slams his hand on the table before saying, "He is bluffing. This cannot really be happening. He wouldn't show it to the world."

General Roshenko: "We must remember what he said about freedom, you have to take this seriously."

As the Russians are watching in horror, the ICBMs land, and huge mushroom clouds are shown forming. Former diplomat Sasha Malinov screams, "This is unbelievable!"

President Baskov yells to his aid, "Ivan, get Cuba on the phone! I want confirmation."

Ivan quickly dials his phone and says, "President Baskov needs confirmation. Can you see evidence of a nuclear attack on the city of Miami?" A few seconds later, with horror in his eyes, he sets down the phone and says, "Sir, this is real. President Gomez just confirmed that two nuclear missiles just landed on Miami." He then looks down, clenches his stomach and mumbles to himself, "I think I'm going to be sick."

President Baskov: "That Jim Taylor is a madman! He *will* destroy us. Get him on the phone, now!"

Ivan summons the strength to pick up the phone and dial. He turns on speaker phone and places the phone in the middle of the table. Jim answers saying, "Hello, President Baskov, I had a feeling I'd be hearing from you right about now."

President Baskov exclaims, "You just obliterated your own city!"

Jim: "Yes, I did, just as I said I would, and in fifty minutes Kazan is next, as I see you're still holding Alaska hostage."

President Baskov: "We are pulling out right now." He voicelessly whispers to General Roshenko, "Get us out now!" General Roshenko gets up and leaves the room immediately, dialing his phone as he leaves. President Baskov then returns to a normal voice and says to Jim, "I am very sorry for this misunderstanding, President Taylor."

"So you'll be out by 1?" Jim quickly replies.

President Baskov: "Yes, definitely!"

Jim: "If you are, then ok, but if not, I will proceed as planned."

President Baskov: "I assure you that it will not be necessary. However, I would like to ask, if you truly believe in freedom, why did your government abandon my country in the 1990s, after you forced us to become a Democracy?"

Jim: "Abandon you?"

President Baskov: "Yes, my people were starving. They waited in lines over two hours a day for food, what there was of it. We had nothing but a desperate struggle for survival, and yet no help from you! We had mass unemployment and grinding poverty, and where was your help? We switched to Democracy as President Reagan forced us to do, but then you left us to die!"

Jim: "We hadn't realized that, but you're absolutely right. We did let your country down, and we let you struggle without any help."

Sasha Malinov shouts, "You are a mean and vicious people, a bully to the world!" The others in the room stare at her in disbelief.

President Baskov quickly exclaims, "I apologize for my advisor's outburst!"

Jim: "I agree with you that we let you down, but us being a bully is a misconception, and I will prove it to you. I intend to make it up to you. America treats her allies well, and I'd like for you to be our ally."

Sasha Malinov: "You have threatened to destroy us and now you want us to be your ally?"

Jim: "I did nothing more than defend my borders. Now that your President is withdrawing from Alaska, as a fellow democratic country, I offer you my hand in friendship and hereby formally invite your country to become an ally of the United States of America. We will protect your borders as we do our own."

Jacob whispers to Jim asking, "Wait, you want to ally with Russia?!" to which Jim simply nods and gives a thumbs up.

President Baskov: "Just like that, you suddenly consider us your friend?"

Jim: "Any friend of freedom is a friend of mine. Join us, and we will be friends. I will send help to your country so that you can learn the positive ways of capitalism. We'll help you set up an economy that will grow and thrive. These are things that we should have done over forty-five years ago. You have my sincere apologies for our having overlooked them."

President Baskov: "You would really do that?"

Jim: "I take care of my friends. Can I count you as one?"

President Baskov: "Of course, I hope that you will come to visit soon. I believe we can learn much from each other."

Jim: "I'm looking forward to it. Rest assured, as of now you are an ally of the United States of America, and any invasion by another country on *your* soil will be seen as an act of war against the United States of America as well as yours. We *will* protect you."

President Baskov: "Very good, I'm glad we reached this understanding."

Jim: "I will be talking more with you later." Jim hangs up the phone. He then tells Jacob, "As President Reagan once said, 'trust but verify.'" He then calls General Maghee and asks, "Is Russia getting out of Alaska?"

General Maghee, chuckling before replying, "Yep, I've never seen a faster military withdrawal! They left everything! They just…left. They put our flag back up, and then turned everything over to Governor Sherman. It must have been Miami."

Jim: "Uh, something like that; we had a nice, long heart-to-heart powwow, and Russia is now our ally."

In confusion, General Maghee asks, "Our *ally*, sir?"

Jim: "Yes, I consider them to be a friend of liberty, and I plan on it making up to them for the wrong we committed when we abandoned them back in the '90s. Think about it, they switched away from communism, and our aid was nowhere in sight."

Later that afternoon, in response to the use of nuclear weapons, an emergency UN meeting is called for the next morning to discuss the recent events that have transpired, namely, Jim Taylor's fracturing of the Utopian Socialists of America and his use of nuclear weapons.

Representatives from all of the UN member countries are present, and given the seriousness of the topic, many of the national leaders have decided to attend personally in this massive hall. At the center of the end wall is the UN moderator, who is standing at a podium hitting his gavel to get everyone's attention before addressing the assembly.

"Thank you all for coming here today. I know we were not scheduled to meet until January, but the events of this past week merit an emergency session. As you know, Jim Taylor of the currently *unrecognized* United States of America has unleashed multiple weapons of mass destruction on the city of Miami. This is in complete disregard to human and animal rights, the health of the environment, and UN authority. Given these grievous actions, three issues are up for a vote today:

"One, whether or not we will recognize the United States of America as a sovereign nation;

"Two, if we do recognize the United States of America as a sovereign nation, then whether or not we should condemn it as a terrorist nation, invade it, and topple Jim Taylor in favor of a more peaceful leader; or

"Three, if we vote against accepting the United States as a sovereign nation, then whether or not we should return it to the Utopian Socialists of America.

"These items are open for discussion, and then we shall take a vote."

Almost before the moderator is done with his introduction, Canadian Prime Minister Tremblay, himself, says very heatedly, "Jim Taylor is completely out of control! If we don't stop him now, what is to keep that madman from attacking all of us? Canada does not recognize the United States of America as a sovereign nation."

A Brazilian representative very quickly chimes in, "Brazil agrees with Prime Minister Tremblay, 100%. Mr. Taylor is a mad man of Hitler proportions!"

Prime Minister John Moore, representing Australia, shouts, "I couldn't have said it better. Jim Taylor is going against everything I stand for, and we need to squash his rebellion, and take measures to ensure this cannot happen again!"

German and French representatives quickly agree saying, "We agree with Canada, Brazil, and Australia." and "He must be stopped!" respectively.

A Chinese representative adds, "China agrees, and we are prepared to use all of our military might to end this madness."

Trying to stop this, Mexican President Rodriguez says, "Jim Taylor is only fighting for freedom! We cannot condemn him for that. Mexico stands with Jim Taylor and the United States."

A Cuban representative then shouts, "He just unleashed multiple nuclear weapons only 140 kilometers from our border, and I am worried about nuclear fallout!"

Isaac says "Everyone, please be calm about this. This very entity, the UN, was created in order to ensure that no world war would ever happen again. Although I agree that Jim Taylor is causing problems, we should not attack him and start a war. We must use the UN as it was intended, for diplomacy; we need to use peaceful negotiations to end this conflict."

The moderator then asks, "But Czar Wolfe, you have the biggest threat. In fact, he stole your own land and attacked your people, with *your* own weapons, and yet you are voting against taking any military action against this man? That is unfathomable!"

Isaac replies, "We *must* stay the course! We are on the verge of becoming a completely utopian society, and a war would derail all of the progress that everyone has made. We *must* stay the course."

The Chinese representative looks directly at Isaac as he quickly responds, "Czar Wolfe, please, let us help you to defend yourself. We could quickly eliminate this threat and enforce peace. All of the other countries except *his* allies agree."

President Baskov chimes in, "You can count Russia as an ally of Jim Taylor. He is a great pioneer for freedom. I vote in favor of Jim Taylor and the United States of America."

Prime Minister Tremblay instantly turns toward President Baskov, and asks, "Are you mad?! You nearly gave me a heart attack when you seized Alaska, and now somehow you two have suddenly become *friends*?"

President Baskov calmly replies, "Eh, we had a little skirmish in the snow. This caused us to engage in some very meaningful talks with President Taylor. He is helping us to establish a healthy, thriving, and prosperous economy. He and the United States of America are our friends, and we will defend them, both here diplomatically, and on the battleground as needed."

Isaac asks, "President Baskov, How could *you, you,* become friends with Jim Taylor?"

President Baskov replies, "I can understand your confusion, but Jim Taylor is actually a really good person, and I completely support him."

In shock, the moderator exclaims, "Well, *this* is an interesting development. Russia is a major nation, with veto power, and so are the Utopian Socialists of America. Um, I guess this is a dead issue, then. I don't think anything good can come from pursuing this further." After he says this, several national leaders and representatives start yelling at each other, resulting in mass chaos. The UN moderator then shouts over the loud speaker and bangs his gavel to try to get people's attention, "Excuse me, excuse me, please! Will everyone please calm down? This is the United Nations. We do not fight here!" His voice gets calmer, as everyone is now listening to him. He continues, "On the contrary, we promote *peace*. This meeting is adjourned." He then hits his gavel to signal the meeting is ended.

END CHAPTER

CHAPTER NINE

THREE MONTHS LATER

The dust has settled and three months have passed. Inside the now thriving Cordonia house, Eva, her mother, and her daughter are sitting at their table eating dinner. This is now a nightly ritual of theirs. Grandma exclaims, "Oh, it's so nice that we can eat Sunday dinner here all together – no more of you working twelve hours every single day!"

Eva happily replies, "Si, Abuela, this is wonderful! All I have to do now is go to school. Czar Wolfe has made great changes."

With a bit of bitterness in her voice Grandma says, "I just wish all the riots would stop and that evil man, Jim Taylor, would stop causing so much trouble. He's trying to get people to revolt against our beloved Czar and our way of life."

Eva sighs before replying, "I don't know what his problem is, other than that he just wants to have more than everyone else."

Grandma: "Some people are just bullies and want to have to more than the rest of us!"

Eva's daughter pulls on Eva's arm as she asks, "Mommy, can I have more chicken?"

With a smile on her face Eva replies, "Sure honey!" before putting another piece of chicken on her daughter's plate.

Moving on to the Nolen family, Mary and Brian are out on a leisurely walk on a sunny fifty-degree day. As they are walking, Brian quietly asks Mary, "Do you think Rick will ever be the same?"

Mary shakes her head and says, "No, Honey, I don't think so. Between the medications and the brain washing, he just isn't the same kid anymore. It's like he's become someone else altogether. I can't believe the government would do this to a child, it's awful! He's lost all emotion; he is nothing more than a zombie…" Her voice trails off for a moment, and then with rage, she exclaims, "It just breaks my heart!"

Mary breaks down crying as she is speaking. They stop walking, and Brian grabs her by the shoulders, looking her in the eyes. Seeing the woman he fell in love with all those years ago, he drops his voice and says, "I swear on my life that somehow, we will escape this God-forsaken country. Then, we'll get the best doctors we can find and get our Rick back! I'm sure we can reverse the damage. There has to be a way!"

Mary looks him in the eyes, seeing the young and impetuous man she fell in love with, and thinks to herself, "You're still not a very good liar, are you?" After a second or two, she regains her composure and says under her breath, "I hope so, but how are we ever going to get out of here? They've taken our house, they've bugged our phones, and we can't do anything without them knowing about it. I'm sure someone is even watching us right now. I've even stopped wearing my jewelry for fear they're spying through them."

Brian takes her by the hand and kisses her forehead, then whispers in her ear, "I know, but I'm working on a plan with the new trains I'm testing. I think I can go for a test run and accidentally end up in the free side of Virginia."

Mary exclaims in a whisper, "Do you think you could actually make that happen?"

Brian whispers back, "They're making it hard, but I think I can do it."

Mary, realizing they might be drawing suspicion, shouts, "Oh, I love it when you talk like that – let's get started right away!" Then they continue on their way.

Now, to check on George, he has found his way further south and is now enrolled in a tech school in Georgia. He is in his dorm room with his roommate Derrick, who is not in a good mood. Derrick whines, "Man, I can't believe you got in here without even finishing high school! My parents almost had to bribe people to get me in here. This is one of the top engineering schools in the country."

George fires back, "Look, Derrick, I worked very hard while I was in high school. I studied, studied, *studied*, to get that perfect ACT score. I *earned* this scholarship and full room and board."

Derrick throws his pen down on his desk, as he says, "I guess so, but I wish I could have skipped my senior year."

George: "I didn't have a choice. I had to! While we were trying to escape the Utopians, my brother got shot in the leg, and I-I-I-I-I I can't even talk to my family! You have no sympathy from me."

Derrick: "You got me there, but it's still not fair."

George retorts, "Dude, nothing in life is fair! You could have aced your ACT and skipped your senior year, too." He sighs before continuing, "At least we're free here."

Derrick: "Georgie, my boy, you are 100% correct, and I love this country!"

Now back to politics. During these last three months people have been acclimating to the changes to their lives. The Utopian leaders are about to have a meeting in the capital, which is still Washington D.C.

Czar Isaac Wolfe enters a large conference room, sits down, and joins his advisors and district leaders. All are now sitting at a large table. When Isaac sees that everyone is paying attention, he starts the meeting by saying, "So, ladies and gentleman, it's been three months since our last full meeting. As you recall, the vote was 9-4 in favor of taking drastic measures, but, as we can clearly see, things have stabilized, just as I knew they would. Things are looking bright, and people are happy. The reeducation centers are working out well, and people have homes and jobs where they only have to work thirty-five hours a week. Truly, we are nearing the Utopia we promised!"

Within a second Alfred Schmidt retorts, shouting, "Sir, we are nowhere close! China has all of our secrets, and I expect them to take us over any day. Our military is even weaker than it was when we began!"

Los Angeles District Leader Tom Rhoades quickly chimes in, "The riots continue in LA. The reeducation centers just are not working fast enough, and Jim Taylor is not helping by fueling people's desire to be free. I was with you three months ago, Isaac, but I cannot be anymore. We have to stop Taylor now!"

Before long Seattle District Leader Tony Sanchez adds, "It's not any better in my region. A lot of the formerly rich techies are not cooperating and continue to want capitalism back, along with a free market economy. It's a mess! Jim Taylor needs to go now, or this will only get worse. I don't know how much longer we can control this."

Soon, the San Francisco District Leader Henry Pilot affirms, "Agreed, the reeducation centers in the Western District are simply not working fast enough."

Somewhat in shock, Isaac asks, "So, all three of you have turned against me as well? Are all eight of my District Leaders against me?"

All eight of the utopian district leaders chime in, nearly in unison, with a chorus of "YES!"

Isaac then asks, "How can this be? Things have stabilized. No more states have seceded, and polls show that 65% of the public is happy, or even ecstatic!"

Alfred Schmidt replies, "Yes, that may be, but the other thirty-five percent, the Jim Taylor lovers, are destroying our nation. We need to stop these revolts and start publicly executing those involved."

In fear and disgust, Isaac rears back before he asks, "That's a little barbaric, don't you think?" After pausing for a second, he continues, saying, "As long as I'm in charge, we will never do that!" He looks around the room with a confused look on his face, and a second later he asks the burning question, "Has everyone lost their mind?"

The Secretary of Housing Samantha Jones looks at Isaac and quickly answers, "I'm still with you. Isaac!" She then looks around at everyone else in the room and says, "I think everyone just needs to calm down and understand that this will take time. Things have stabilized, and we are making progress, with sixty-five percent of us living the Utopian Dream. In time, we can make that one hundred percent. Then, as Isaac has promised, we can start this movement in the states that have seceded, and they will come around and join us."

Somewhat cheered up, Isaac continues, "Yes, they all will. Then, one by one, every *country* will join us. Eventually, the whole world will, and we will be a united, utopian society, where everyone is equal, and everyone has all of their needs met. All will be happy in this remarkable Utopian World. The dream is this close" he motions with his fingers, "to being a reality and it's because of us. We should be proud!"

Dumbfounded by what he perceives as 'stupidity,' Alfred Schmidt stands up and roars, "You are a delusional madman! Soon, we will be taking orders from the Chinese." he pounds his fist on the table, "They must go," he pounds his fist on the table again, "Jim Taylor must go," he pounds his fist on the table a third time, "and *you* must go!!!!" and then he storms out of the room.

Once Alfred Schmidt has left the room, Isaac calmly says, "For the record, effective immediately Alfred is no longer a district leader. Let's get him to a reeducation center." Isaac then looks at Matthew and says, reassign him." He then looks around at everyone in the room and says, "You can all be replaced if need be. I will not let our Utopian Dream die!" He then gets up and continues, "I'm giving a speech tonight to unite this country, and I want all of you there. This speech is going to be broadcast, but I want the audience to be made up of the leadership our country and I want everyone to be united. We will then meet back here tomorrow at 8 am to discuss our steps to move forward to unite the world into a complete Utopian Society."

Isaac leaves the room, and shortly thereafter, everyone else does as well.

That evening Jim and Jacob are sitting at a table in an office of the former governor's mansion, now presidential mansion. There is a TV on in the background, as Jim and Jacob are going over various reports. The table is flooded with papers; the time is 7:55 pm. Jim, needing a break, sets down the financial report he was going over and says to Jacob, "Jacob, can you believe that it's only been three months since the election? It seems like it was years ago!"

Jacob, still reading a paper, replies, "It's been so stressful – worth it, but stressful!"

Jim: "Yes, and things are finally stabilizing now. We've even managed to move out most, if not all, of the Utopians. We have a new, stable money supply, and the economy is thriving. There is plenty of food and oil here, and, thanks to Mexico, clothing as well. Diplomatically, Russia is now our best friend. Our military is growing stronger every day, and China understands that we can take out their satellite system and will destroy them if they try to invade any of our states. I've also let them know that spying is an act of war. All in all, life is good. Let the Utopians be Utopians! I'm glad to have that element out of our society. The Utopian Socialists have been holding us back for over a hundred years."

Jacob puts down the paper he was reading and says, "All that is true, but we do still have the poor to worry about. With five percent unemployment and fifteen percent of the people living in poverty, American kids are going to bed hungry, and we're being blasted by the UN on this. The Russian delegates have been asking me how we are going to help *their* poor when we're not even helping our own."

Jim: "Agreed, Isaac does have some good points. Capitalism fails the poor, but it's the best system for the good of all. Unfortunately, the poor are just collateral damage. We need families and churches to help their own poor, and until the Stock Market Crash of 1929 and the Dust Bowl that hit shortly thereafter, that was the way of doing things in the United States. The churches and family members did take care of the poor people. When that happens, then capitalism is flawless."

Jacob yawns before asking, "But how do we change the culture? People just don't help others in need anymore, basically since the FDR administration brought in all the welfare programs. People didn't *need* to help others under the socialistic way of life. Currently, they don't know how or even that they should."

Jim replies, "Oh, I don't know about that. Since the split, the people of the United States have shown that they are capable of great kindness. If we encourage this, we can start changing that socialistic attitude, one person at a time. One good deed starts another, then another, and so on. I plan on giving a speech on this next week, outlining a plan for new tax incentives for all who give to charities, on both the business and personal levels."

Jacob: "That's a great idea! When Isaac took office eight years ago, all tax breaks were eliminated in favor of a tax-and-spend system."

Jim: "This will work, as it did before, but we need to be diligent. We can't allow the tax code to become so complicated that it takes years off a person's life just by trying to figure out which forms to fill out. Also, Congress needs to continue working only part time and for little or nothing, as our forefathers did, and I want to encourage charity workers to do the same, so that people will not be afraid to give their money to help out the neediest among us. Everything has worked out well for us thus far, and there is no reason why this won't work, too."

Jacob starts looking around the room and sees the TV. He notices that Isaac is at a podium, about to speak. There is a large blue curtain behind him. Jacob immediately shouts, "Hey look, Isaac is giving a speech."

Jim looks at the TV and says with a smile on his face, "Turn it up. Things are going so well, maybe he's conceding!"

Jacob grabs the TV remote and turns up the volume. Isaac begins speaking before a crowd of his country's Utopian leaders, saying, "Good evening, ladies and gentleman of this great Utopian Socialist America! I thank you for all of your patriotism over the past three months. It has been a long three months," and suddenly, the TV goes out.

Meanwhile, at the podium Isaac continues his speech uninterrupted, unaware that the broadcast signal was cut, "with many obstacles from the rebels led by Jim Taylor, but we have managed to weather the storm. Utopia is at an all time high. Polls show that over sixty-five percent of us are happy, if not ecstatic. I want to thank each and every one of you for keeping our dreams alive and for keeping our children's dreams alive. We are well on our way to a perfect world!" Just then, Alfred Schmidt comes out from behind the curtain and walks up behind him, interrupting Isaac's speech. Isaac covers the microphone and whispers to him, "Excuse me, please, Alfred, I'm not done yet."

Alfred Schmidt says without emotion, "Yes, yes, you are." Schmidt puts a gun to Isaac's back and pulls the trigger. As Isaac is falling down, Schmidt pushes him to the right, and walks up to the podium.

As Isaac is bleeding out, Alfred begins to speak to the audience. This is inaudible to Isaac, who is left watching, knowing that he is about to die. The crowd begins to cheer about something Schmidt just said. Isaac closes his eyes and begins to cry, thinking to himself, "All I wanted was for the world to be a better place..."

TO BE CONTINUED